Freddie Gavin

I0451666

Cover Photo © 2018 by Lakishia Dinkins

Edited by: Laurie Trott-Spivey, Patrice & Rebecca Walker, &
Alyssa Harris

Published by: Freddie G Publications & Trott Publications

ISBN: 978-0-692-91744-2

1

DEDICATIONS and Thank you(s)

As a first-time author there are several people I would like to thank. I first want to thank Olivia Gavin for always encouraging me. We have been married for a few years now, 30, and she is the true writer and the smartest person in the Gavin clan. I also let her know that she is without a doubt the smartest person that I know.

I like to thank my mom, Irene Smith: One of the sweetest and most caring person anyone could have as a mother, May She Forever RIP.

I would like to thank my DAD, Freddie Gavin Sr.: One of the coolest-level-headed persons that I know. He is great listener and although his memory is fading, he has a sense of humor that will keep anybody upbeat, he is also my movie partner.

I would like to thank my three wonderful children, daughter, Dequilla Renee Gavin and My two sons, Marcus and Kyle Gavin. Words can't express how much I love you guys. I also would like to thank my grandchild, Harmony Gavin. She keeps Olivia and I grounded.

Lastly, I dedicated this book to all the characters in the book. Although their names have been slightly changed, I did rely heavily on my friendships with a few of them and our experiences together to help complete the missing pieces from my dream to write this book.

Table of Contents

Freddie Gavin

Willie Lynch Was My Friend

"When White is right and things seem bright

Spend a day in my shoes

When times are hard and justice flawed

Spend a day in my shoes

When work is bleak and employment's peaked

Spend a day in my shoes

When nothing's right because of civil rights plight

Spend a day in my shoes

A DAY IN MY SHOES, YOU WILL NOT MUMBLE

A DAY IN MY SHOES, WILL MAKE YOU HUMBLE

A DAY IN MY SHOES, YOUR EYES WILL OPEN

TO INJUSTICE WAYS OF AFRICAN-AMERICANS PAST,
PRESENT MISFORTUNES!"

(Freddie Gavin December 2011)

Chapter 1

LIFE

It was a cold winter day in Springfield, Illinois when Senator

Obama stood before thousands of excited Illinoisans and announced

he was running for President of the United States. The young

senator from Chicago, by way of Hawaii, and Kenya, where Tea

Party members suggest his true national origin lies, knew the

significance of his announcement. He also knew this announcement

paralleled another great Chicagoan senator who would go on to

become, in some historians' and American minds, one of the greatest

Presidents in U.S. history.

President Lincoln, the "dogmatic deity" who freed the slaves

(although there is literature that opposes this claim, it looks good in

history books), would press the issue of racial injustice. This iconic

President was a self-made, poor man's politician, who would later

believe his journey of humanity would not be complete without the

idea that all men should be equal. He was a man who was

empathetic to the plight of the Black man. He could not have

expressed his abhorrence for the treatment of the Black man any

better than in the 1865 letter he wrote to abolitionist, Frederick

Douglass. This letter would be the first to the abolitionist to show

respect and address the rights of black men as a vital part of the

American fabric.

The senator from Chicago, Barrack "Barry" Obama, wanted to

expound upon the political God-like figure's ideology of making "all

citizens" free from injustices and any type of tyranny that kept

Americans divided. The simple idea that all people should truly be

equal is the mantra which the Constitution of the United States so

eloquently and metaphorically speaks.   If the 45-year-old Obama

became president, not only would he be one of the youngest to hold

the office, but he would also become the nation's first African–

American President of the United States. Where Lincoln once called

on a divided house to stand together, and where common hopes and

common dreams still live, the first term senator wanted to enhance

the 16th President's thesis on the divisiveness of American inequality

and racial divide. The senator from Illinois believed, like the 16th

President, that ALL Americans given the opportunity could live in the most powerful nation in the world free from economic and racial injustice. His idea was based on an idea of hope and change.

I knew the senator—well—I knew him not because we grew up together, but because we were only two of a few African-Americans at one of the nation's oldest and prestigious institutions. We studied different disciplines but sometimes we would get together with the few other black faces on campus and talk about life as Harvard students. My first impression of him was like any other black face in a predominantly white institution—excited to see another black face, but driven with anxiety and reluctance because of the unknown expectation. As I spent what little time I had with the future senator and now President, I knew he was special. His being special had a lot to do with the fact that he truly was considered an African-American. His father was an African from Kenya and his mother was a white woman from Kansas. Although issues with his identity have been documented, I believe it was this inner confusion that made him special. I also knew he was destined for something. At that time, I didn't know what the something was—but I knew the something was either going to be very good or very bad. I guess my "special gift" wasn't developed enough to identify good or bad, but he would later go on and become the 44th President of the United States.

In the late 70s and early 80s it was rare for an ambitious black boy like me from West Virginia, or a gifted mind destined for greatness like Obama, to even think about applying to an Ivy League school like Harvard. I guess the Civil Rights Movement bridged the gap and reshaped some of its ideas of equality from the southern Jim Crow, whites-only principle of inequality. The school's admissions office must have concluded that this elite, Northern Ivy-League school would be better equipped if it had a little color. I'm sure someone at Harvard must have realized, "It was the North who fought and died for the freedom of the slaves." That same someone must have fostered a constitutional creed that stated ALL PERSONS had a right to a great education, even if that person happens to be Black—queue Barrack and me.

I have always excelled in school. Not because I wanted to, but because of the pressure that was put on my brother and me from our parents—especially my mother, who we affectionately nicknamed, "The Professor." I can hear my mother asking my brother and me, "How was school, and what did you learn today?" In unison, we would always say in a long apathetic voice, "School was fine—and we learned everything." She would always push the envelope and ask, "What does FINE mean?" Out of her sight my brother and I would quietly fight over who was going to challenge the Professor in a sort of open-air debate of word Scrabble, or Jeopardy, minus Alex Trebek.

I can recall, just like it was yesterday, my brother and I in our room talking about boxing. Most people believed that Muhammad Ali was the greatest fighter to ever grace the sport of boxing. In those days, the early 70s, there was no such thing as the internet, or iPhones where at the click of a finger, you couldn't Google any information you wanted to. If you wanted information in those days, you would have to get it from a book. Your family would have to be like our family with a large collection of books—or you would go down to the local library and check a book out. If you were lucky like my brother and me, you would get it from the local barbershop where all the African-American men would meet religiously on a Saturday morning—even if you weren't getting a haircut. Sometimes, if we were real lucky, we could get information on the T.V., but that was very rare—the Professor didn't play that. I always kid with my mom to this day that we believed T.V. served only one purpose, which was to let us know if we were going to war, or to let us know that the President or some type of important political leader had died. Watching T.V. just to watch it was a very rare thing in our house. And to this day, my brother and I own maybe a T.V. just to entertain guests. I have to have a few T.V.'s, especially when my dumbass friends grace me with their presence at my place.

Anyway, I believed Ali was the greatest! My brother for some reason liked Smoking Joe Frazier. I think he liked him more because he hated Ali's narcissistic attitude. I guess he didn't understand that Ali's antics and being a bragger were just bluster—all a stunt to get people excited about his up and coming match. In real life, Joe and Ali were good friends. Many reports would later suggest that Joe lent Ali money during the time Ali was locked up for refusing to be drafted in the military. What I thought was a

11

brilliant rant about his refusal to enter the military, and Ali being Ali, stated and believed that African-Americans had no business fighting other people of color. Ali would state that, "Why in the hell would I go fight against my Asian brothers 10,000 miles away that didn't do anything to me, when I live in a country where my white brothers won't even let me use the front door of a restaurant, sit and eat at the same table as other white brother and sisters?" Ali was not only a fighter, but he also was one of the leaders in the African-American community, especially as it related to the many injustices that they faced.

In Ali's heyday, he really didn't have any challengers to dethrone him from the heavy weight division. Here comes Joe Frazier. A five foot, eleven inch, muscular, bulldog-mean as hell fighter out of Philadelphia, Pennsylvania, by way of South Carolina, who would whip Ali's ass in what was known as "The Fight of The Century." Joe did little talking, but backed it up with his fist. Everyone pitted Ali as the Civil Rights Champion. Ali, against the white man's champion, the Uncle Tom, Frazier. It's noted that Ali, through his funny-smooth talking-rhymes and trash talking rhythmical interviews with his buddy Howard Cosell, turned many African-Americans against Joe. Joe didn't like this, but he understood who Ali was. These two fighters throughout the years said many negative things about each other, but they revered each other in the ring. They respected each other's talent as boxers and respected each other as black men in the 50s and 60s during the height of segregation. Later in life they would go on to become close friends. Ali would attend the private funeral service for Frazier in Philadelphia.

So, I guess my brother and I were just trying to debate about the flavor of the day. And since boxing was one of those hot topics in the 70s, we picked a side. I chose Ali and my brother chose Frazier. As we debated back and forth about which fighter was the best, we never realized that the Professor was eavesdropping outside of our door. Mom loved to listen in on us debating back and forth and she would later admit to us that when we debated, it sounded like two men laying out their arguments in a clear and precise position. So, one day when the Professor was listening, she overheard me use a few words in a statement that she knew I should not have known.

Maybe it was the content in which I made my statement, but she knew. She also knew that since I was older than my brother, I was trying to impress him and throw him off so I would have the upper hand when we debated.

"Jeffery, man, you know I'm right about this—Ali is gonna kill Frazier!"

"Man, what you talking about—have you seen the muscles on Frazier? Ali can't do nothing but dance and punch and it don't even seem like he is punching hard—it looks like he runs the whole fight."

"When is the fight again?"

"I think they are fighting early March—that's the word."

The fight information would always come out in the black community long before they start advertising it on T.V. or radio. We didn't have an exact date, but we would know that these two titans would be fighting sometime in March.

"Well, I don't care what day, or when it is, Ali is gonna destroy Frazier!"

"Who is Frazier anyway—he's not known!" Jeffery didn't care if Ali was fighting Mr. Turnupseed, a neighbor who lived around the corner from us, he wasn't cheering for Ali.

"Man EJ, Frazier is a good fighter, plus he's younger than Ali."

"I think Frazier is gonna knock Ali out!"

"Boy, please!"

This went back and forth for hours. Now, I had to get clever and start trying to use big words to sound smart. "Jeffery, you have nothing to substantiate Frazier's victory, just bluster!"

"And—what facts do you have, EJ, except for a whole lotta trash talking." Jeffery was kinda right. These guys had never fought before. The only thing we knew about them were previous fights against other opponents and what everyone was saying, and most of the time they were wrong. The verdict was out. Half of the black community loved Ali, and the other half loved Frazier. The difference was that Ali was a proven champion and Frazier was the new kid on the block.

"So tell me EJ—what round do you think your guy will lose in?" Trying to be funny, and just like that, Jeffery replied.

15

"My guy will lose in the 18th round."

He knew that there weren't 18 rounds; he was also trying to be funny.

"In fact, EJ, your guy will win, but only when he interviews with his buddy Howard Cosell—shucking and jiving—but this time with two black and swollen eyes and some busted ribs—so he will win the talking game."

"But—he still will be pretty." We both just laughed. Now I was trying to go in for the kill.

"Jeffery," in my New England upper class voice, "Ali shows such equanimity in the ring. His charisma, carte blanche with the ability to display an élan of Machiavellian, without being too maudlin as he triumphs to victory is why he will be the victor."

The door opened and the Professor was standing there looking at me like I had done the most horrible thing in the world.

"Boy, what are you talking about? Why are you trying to use words in a conversation you having with your brother as if you won the Nobel Peace Prize in literary work? Using big words don't make you smart or seem smart—in fact, it makes you sound like you don't know what you are talking about—you guys are talking about BOXING!"

"Stop being glib!"

"Look it up!"

The Professor left our room as she came. We both started laughing.

"Now what were you saying—Einstein?" Jeffery said.

We both laughed again.

I quietly suggested that I still thought Ali would win the first fight, which became the Fight of the Century—Ali lost! My mother was a wonderful person and to date, she still reads and continue to challenge my brother and me even as older men. Sometimes I won— and sometimes, he would win, but in all, the Professor had the upper hand.

My mother was a beautiful, thoughtful, loving and God fearing homemaker. However, the full majesty of her beauty was more internal than external. Sure, she had stunning outward beauty that caught my dad's eye, and probably other suitors who didn't get the opportunity of having her as a wife, but the reality of what made my mother special to her family and friends was her deep love for us.

The Professor's intellect was unmatched—if her friends and family needed answers about anything, they knew who to call. Remember, these were the days before Gates and Zuckerberg paved the way to the world's multi-media highway of social utopia. She was the first in her family to attend and graduate college. Now as an adult, her mission in life, other than reading anything she could get her hands on, was providing a safe haven for my dad, brother and me--her boys. Making sure her boys had everything we needed to be successful throughout our day drove my mom. If mom was happy, the whole house was happy; and when my mom was sad or mad, the whole house was concerned.

Irene Smith Truman or Ren-ee (The ee's were long and this is what family and friends called her for short) knew almost everything—she was like a librarian in a library. My dad would always say she was the smartest person he knew. Mom would always tell my brother and me that she read to us while we were in her womb so there was no surprise as to why my brother and I excelled in school (well, I still think my brother is a little slow.). My mother read everything, and my brother and I were the recipients of forced reading, which we hated but would eventually grow to appreciate. Mom had this thing where she woke up early before my brother and I woke for school and find some type of article she had found from a magazine, or newspaper, or even a quote from a book. She would then paste this article on our mirror in the bathroom. These teaching tools (which is what I liked to call them) would be visible for both of us to see when we brushed our teeth for school. There was no getting around reading the article she had left us, because we had to discuss the article during dinner when dad came home from work and our school work was done. These little morning "assignments" are how she got the nickname the Professor.

George Abraham Lincoln Truman, my dad, was a typical black man in the 60s and 70s. One day, I asked my granny why dad had so many first names. Granny told me in her high pitched voice, "Well, EJ, George was my father's name and your father looks just like him, bless his soul. Uh—I named him Abraham Lincoln because

Lincoln hated slavery and freed the slaves. Did you know that, EJ? Did you know Lincoln freed the slaves?"

"Yes, ma'am." I didn't want to let granny know her version of Lincoln's abhorrence of slavery was a little flawed, but considering the source, we tend to accept the views of people about life when they get old and a little senile, especially if it's a loved one. I figured Truman must have come from Harry Truman. My mind began to wonder about Harry Truman— "Let's see—grew up around racism—check, paid ten dollars to be a member of the KKK—check, and became President of the United States—WOW!" But, I also knew he had somewhat of a credible campaign against racial injustice—although, laissez-faire—but he had one. So, I can kind of accept Truman as a last name. And let's face it, being in America as a black person, you would inherit a European name.

Anyway, Dad worked hard all day, never complained about much and relied on my mother for almost everything. I can't ever recall a time when I saw my dad cry, or even yell. I do know his word was law and all he needed to do to my brother and I when we were misbehaving was give us a hard stare and we knew to straighten up.

20

My dad was a self-made man. This was rare in the south where Jim Crow basically defined your lot in life, especially as a business owner. He had his own construction business and was involved in the community. I think he was some type of community leader, but I never did ask him about that. All of the kids and adults in the neighborhood loved my dad. He was sort of a creature of habit. Every day on his way home from a job he and his team were working on, he would stop at the local store and buy a few bags of candy, and in his own rendition of ghetto Santa Claus, handed it out to the little kids and teens that were in the neighborhood. He would always ask each kid about school and their families.

George Abraham Lincoln Truman, a hard-working man from Alabama. A towering figure in statue. A Leroy Brown, like from the Jim Croce song, "Leroy Brown." However, he was a family man—a kind man, a man that every guy in the neighborhood wanted to be, and a man that white men revered. He was also a momma's boy. My dad grew up a poor sharecropper's son, who learned the scores of working and taking care of his family. A very soft-spoken man, he had a look that told you exactly what was on his mind.

However, he had a million dollar smile that made him look like a print face model. His smile was infectious and when people saw him, it made them feel comfortable.

George stood about 6 foot 4 inches tall, with a body like a linebacker. He had a kindness that even the devil could appreciate. I never saw my dad say anything bad about anyone. Even when things weren't going the best for him as a contractor, he never had a negative thing to say about the people who would not hire him for the job. He was a God-fearing man and God always seemed to make things happen for him.

George loved his family and adored his wife. He couldn't believe that she chose him as a mate. However, George was a focused man. There have been many women who tried to take the job of being Mrs. Truman, even before mom came into the picture, but George only had eyes for one. He knew mom was the one for him the first time he laid eyes on her. Everything he did in life as a married man was for the love of his family, especially his wife Renee. They were a perfect earthly match made in heaven—and everyone knew it.

My dad loved his family and he loved his neighborhood. If neighbors needed something fixed, dad would fix it. If a neighbor needed dad to talk with a kid because he or she wasn't listening to a parent, dad would talk to the young person. I can remember Ms. Stanley from around the corner having a problem with her son wanting to join a gang. Tony Stanley was a little guy who thought a gang would be the answer. Tony was a few years older than me. I remember him being small in stature, with a chip on his shoulder. He never really fit in with the crowd, so he thought because he was unpopular and a constant target for bullies, hooking up with a gang was his only option. Tony was a smart young man, but grew tired of giving up himself and whatever money he had to some of the local teenagers who were in school and part of a local gang. Tony believed the only way he could rid himself of these dudes was to join them in gang activity or seek revenge on the mistreatment he regularly received from them. He was fed up. He had to do something or he knew the ass whippings and the insults would continue to plague him throughout his high school years—and probably beyond.

One day, Ms. Stanley came over to our house—I believe it was Good Friday, just before Easter Sunday. She was frantic. There was a knock at the door.

"Hello?"

You could hear a woman crying outside of the door.

"Hello!"

It was about nine o'clock pm and we were all in our rooms. If you listened hard enough you could hear Grandma snoring.

"KNOCK, KNOCK, KNOCK." Dad was asleep, but mom kept saying hello at the door as if the door was going to answer her back. Mom finally opened the door after it woke up the house, minus Dad and Grandma. When she opened the door, Ms. Stanley embraced mom and wouldn't stop crying.

"Nessa—Nessa, what's wrong gurl?" Ms. Stanley kept crying.

"Calm down baby, it's gonna be alright—what's wrong!?" You would have thought someone had died.

"It's Tony!"

"What's wrong with Tony?"

"He left the house with my pistol saying he ain't taking no mo'
shit from them dudes."

"What dudes baby?"

"The gang members that have been messing with him in school.
I'm so afraid that he will hurt someone."

Mom left her downstairs and woke dad.

"Wha--whas up, baby?" he asked, coming out of a deep sleep.

"It's Nessa."

"What's wrong with Nessa."

"It's her boy—he done took her gun and left the house mad,
talking about killing some gang member."

As mom was telling dad the problem Ms. Stanley was having, he
had almost finished putting on his clothes. Dad knew if mom woke
him for whatever reason, something was going on, and most of the
time it wasn't good.

"Where Nessa at?" he asked.

"She's downstairs."

Dad walked downstairs and before he said a word, he put his arms around her and embraced her to let her know that everything was going to be all right.

"Where is Tony?" He asked.

"George I'm not sure—he didn't say where he was going."

"O.K." Even though my dad was tired, I knew he wouldn't rest until he found Tony and made sure that he was O.K. For about an hour, dad searched places and asked around the neighborhood and some of the local hot spots where African-Americans hung out, but to no avail. Before he was to make his last ditch effort and go to where the local gang members hung out, he went over to Penkerton Park. Penkerton Park was where a lot of the kids would go to play basketball at night, or just hang out talking about things that they were planning on doing in life, or even for the weekend.

As he approached the park, he noticed a young man near the bleachers by the baseball field pacing back and forth. Even though some of the lights on the poles that were there to illuminate the field were either burned out, or broken from kids throwing rocks at them, he could visually see that the kid pacing was Tony. He walked up to

26

Tony and saw that he was sweating, breathing sporadically, and had what seemed like a weapon in his hand.

"Tony—what's up, man?"

Tony saw that it was my dad and said, "Hey, Mr. T!" That's what the neighborhood kids called dad.

"What's going on, son? Your mom came by and said you had problems with some local kids."

Even though dad saw the weapon in Tony's hand, he never asked him for it or inquired about it.

"Yes, sir."

"So what you gonna do about it?"

"I got plans."

"O.K. You know where they are now?"

"Yes sir." Even though Tony was upset, he still showed deference to my dad by calling him sir.

"O.K—let's go get them."

Tony seemed confused when dad suggested that he was all down for going to help him get the culprits of his many ass whippings.

"Oh—Mr. T—I really didn't want to involve anyone with my plans."

27

"Son, you are from my side of the tracks and if anyone has a problem with you—then they are going to have a problem with me."

Tony was surprised at what dad said, but he also knew that my dad was the same guy who would bring candy to all the neighborhood kids and would always tell them that if they needed anything or needed him he would always be there. So I guess Tony realized that dad was serious when he suggested that he was going to be his ride-or-die on this mission of revenge.

"Mr. T—aw—O.K." Tony really didn't know what to say.

Dad put both hands on the little guy and looked him in the eyes and said, "Son—there are two things I want you to know before we go seeking revenge. One, if you are planning on using a gun to seek your vengeance because you were bullied, when you pull the trigger and kill someone, you can't bring them back; and two, if you need a gun to show how tough you are, then you need to join the police force, or the military when you get out of high school. What are you going to do with the weapon, son?"

Tony looked at dad, started crying and gave him the weapon. After about 30 minutes or so, Tony had gotten himself together, dad looked at Tony and said, "Let's go."

Although Tony thought dad was taking him home, dad took him right into the lion's den. Not only did my dad have a reputation in our neighborhood, but everyone in our small community knew him. Some knew him as Mr. Truman, some as Truman, the barbershop crew knew him as George, or Big George. The kids in the neighborhood knew him as Mr. T. But most knew him as a guy who was kind, caring and didn't take any shit from anyone, even some kids from a local gang.

"Mr. T, I thought we were going home?" Tony was nervous because he saw that he was where the gang hung out.

"No son, we got a problem—so we are going to fix it."

Dad drove by where some kids were shooting the breeze and he asked Tony if any of those guys were the guys. Tony reluctantly said, "Yeah, that's two of them."

Dad pulled his car over. He looked at Tony and thought about me and my brother and told him, "Let's go."

They got out of the car and walked over to the guys.

"What's up, guys?"

In unison, everyone mumbled what up, or something to that affect.

"You two little niggas know my guy Tony." Dad not only talked the language, he only addressed the two guys that Tony recognized.

"Yeah, I know him." One of the guys said,

Dad looked at the guy that was man enough to say he knew Tony and said, "Cool—which one of you guys are first? Or I will take on all of you."

The guys looked kind of dumbfounded. One of the guys who had no idea what dad was talking about asked, "Sir, what are you talking about?"

"Well, my guy has been having problems at school— the two niggas that are standing by you are two of the ones who have been giving my guy a hard time—because they don't want to go to school to learn, they feel that it is necessary to bully my guy." Dad kept addressing Tony as his guy—like he was trying to sound cool. "So since they want to be bullies and you can clearly see that he is a small guy and it takes a few guys to bully him, I decided to come and clear the air."

The two dudes that dad was talking about were looking away and even Tony could see that they were scared. Tony couldn't believe that these tough guys were now acting like little bitches and dad hadn't even thrown a punch, or shown that he had a weapon. One of the guys who didn't have anything to do with it said, "Sir, I think you need to leave." He pulled his shirt to the side to show that he had a weapon.

Dad saw that he had a weapon and asked again, "Which one of you guys are first—or I will take on all four of you with your guns and anything else you have."

The guy that was showing the gun reached for it, but before he could grab it, dad grabbed his hand, put it in a twist lock and relieved him of his weapon. Before his three friends could respond, dad pulled the young man to the ground and pointed the weapon at one of the guys who had been bullying Tony. "Show your hands!" The other dudes held their hands high in the air. Even though they were part of a gang, this was the first time that the tables had been turned on them where they were the victims.

"Tony, pat them down and if they got guns take them from them."

"Yes, sir." Tony began to pat the other three guys down. Dad had his knee on the small of the back of the guy he just disarmed. The young man that dad disarmed was crying in agony from the arm twist—plus dad had broken his shoulder as he was taking him down to the ground.

Tony patted the other three young men down and found two handguns on two of the guys. He also found a set of brass knuckles and a knife on the guy who didn't banish a gun. Dad thought to himself, "What the hell is this world coming to—where everyone has to have a weapon, or need to show how tough they are, especially in the segregated south."

"Tony, put the weapons in the trunk of my car—the keys are in the ignition." Before Tony left the scene to follow dad's instructions, dad told Tony to make the young men lay down with their hands interlocked in the small of their back. They all followed

32

Tony's instructions. Dad did this so he could show Tony what it felt like to be in control.

"Son, how is your arm?"

"I think you broke it."

"You will live."

Tony did as dad instructed and when he returned from securing the weapons something happened that made this encounter interesting. The boys knew if dad reported what had happened, all these young men would get arrested for multiple felony charges. He knew that and the young men knew that. Dad instructed the young men who were laying down to sit up. He then took his knee off of the young man's back who he just slammed to the ground, breaking his collar bone, and told him to also sit up. He told the kid with the broken shoulder to use his other arm to support the broken arm.

"O.K. fellows, now—are we finished being tough guys?" They all said yes sir as if dad was a drill instructor. "Here's the deal, none of you will ever mess with, bully or attack my guy again—right?"

"Yes sir."

Dad knew that the young man with the broken collar bone needed medical attention, but since he was the ring leader, he needed to make an example out of him and let him stay in pain for a few minutes.

"I don't care what gang you guys are in—don't want to know—but I will be checking on my guy at school to make sure he doesn't have any problems from you guys. Now—I need all of you guys to come with me."

They were confused—why would they go with this crazy old man? But, gang members are like this sometimes. They are tough in their hood until someone tougher than them show up, i.e. the police, military, or in this case Mr. T, my dad.

They all piled into dad's car and dad took the young man to the hospital. He checked the young man in and he and all of the young men waited on their friend in the waiting room. Dad explained to the doctor that the young man had fallen and he brought him to the hospital. Because gangs have a "no snitch" policy, dad knew his lie would be enough. After the young man was feeling better, dad took the young men to one of the local twenty-four hour restaurants and

34

they sat down for a bite to eat. For the next few hours, these young men didn't feel like gang members, but young men hanging out laughing and having a good time with an old dude that cared. He dropped them off later that night. They all got out of the car, except the young man with the repaired collarbone.

"Where do you stay son?"

"I stay with my grandma, up the road." He reluctantly said to my dad.

"O.K." They got to his house and dad escorted him to the door. "I need to speak with your grandma."

Again reluctantly, because in his mind, he thought his grandma had no idea he was involved in a gang. He was afraid that dad was going to expose him, but he realized that he put himself in this situation, so he listened to dad and his grandma's conversation.

Dad introduced himself and what struck the young man was that dad did not expose him. In fact, dad told her the same lie he had told the doctor. The young man was impressed and looked at my dad in a different light.

"Son, I won't tell you to stay out of trouble, but what I will tell you is—be safe."

"Yes, sir."

Dad knew that he would never see this young man again. And this young man knew that dad was a man that, if in another life, he could look up to. A few years later, dad learned that this young man was stabbed to death.

Dad drove Tony home and Nessa was pleased to see that her young man was safe. Nessa thanked dad and told Tony he didn't have to fear no man.

"Son—I told you I will be here for you—you don't have to fear no one especially with a gun. If you gonna take a gun with you to settle a score, you better damn well be willing to use it! It's not worth it, Tony—you are smarter than that." Soon after, dad was back home getting back in his bed.

That's the kind of man my dad was. He was a lawyer, preacher, carpenter and any other profession you could name. We were probably one of a few black families in our neighborhood that had both parents. A lot of the single parent homes showed reverence to my father because he worked hard, loved his family and community, and always had a smile on his face. Although he wasn't educated like mom, or by the world definition of education, he was an extremely intelligent man. He would always tell my brother and me, "Hard work doesn't kill you, but not working will."

The most exciting days as a young man were Saturday mornings. Saturday mornings, my brother and I would wake to the smell of the Professor's cooking and after breakfast, head out to the barbershop with dad. Like clockwork, around seven in the morning, we would arrive at Ashley's Barbershop for our weekly haircuts. Mom wouldn't expect us back until about the time she was fixing lunch. Ashley's was the neighborhood barbershop, owned and operated by Dexter Dillinger. Besides my mom, Mr. Dillinger was the second smartest person my dad knew. He was a tall thin man; very light-skinned with freckles. Mr. Dillinger spoke with an elegance that reminded you of someone standing in front of a few elite trying to solicit money to fund a project. He was an ex-Navy man and boy did he have stories. He used to joke to everybody how secret his missions were, "You guys know if I tell y'all about what happened over there I'm gonna have to kill everyone in my shop—and then I won't have any damn customers." Most of the guys would laugh and call bullshit on Dillinger's missions—but for us boys, we thought he was serious. That's why I liked Saturdays. Besides my mom's Saturday biscuits, molasses and country ham, my brother and I got the chance to go to the barbershop with dad and listen to the old guys talk about everything from religion to politics.

Every now and then the old patrons would interject my brother and me into their deep conversations. The barbershop is the place where I like to say I got my first PhD. There was nothing more exhilarating than being pulled into grown men conversations and saying something that made them say, "Man—young fellow, that was deep." Mr. Piper, one of the barbershop patrons would always tell my dad, "George you got a little Einstein." It always made my dad proud to hear older men express their fondness of me and my brother's intellect. Dad would always give credit to my mom.

"Man, it didn't come from me—that's all Renee."

And in unison, the guys in the barbershop would mutter, "Yeah, Renee is smart as hell." Some of the guy's would joke with my dad and say, "Duke, (Some of the guys who grew up with my dad would call him Duke) how in the hell did your dumb ass pull a fine and smart lady like Renee?"

He would always laugh and say, "Well you know—hehehehe—when you got it, you got it." It made me proud I was among the ghetto elite and they treated my brother and me in a sort of a grown-up way. For the most part, I had a pretty good upbringing. When I got older, I realized although we didn't have much wealth, what we did have would make us the strong men we would eventually become.

Chapter 2

COMING OF AGES

"Welcome to W.E.B. De Bois graduating class of 1979

invocation." This was the sign posted on the school's outside

billboard, and from the looks of it, someone couldn't spell.

"Hello and welcome everyone. My name is principal Dunbar and

I would like to welcome faculty, students, parents, and distinguished

guests to W.E.B Du Bois' graduating class of 1979." At least

principal Dunbar said the school's name right. I'm still wondering

who in their right mind would have let someone spell an icon like

W.E.B. Du Bois name wrong on the billboard for all the world to

see. You would think at least someone from the faculty, or at least

the English department would have seen the misspelling, hell—the

billboard is right next to the teacher's parking lot. I guess I'm

starting to sound and act like the "Professor."

Another thing that was always interesting to me was that for some

reason they always named a school that is predominantly black after

40

some American Black icon. It seems as if they did this to suggest slavery was over and black people needed to stop complaining so much.

I was in a graduating class of 300. There were 3 whites, 12 Hispanics, and 285 blacks—well, we only had 240 blacks graduating. I was valedictorian and my parents couldn't have been more excited. I could see how proud they were by their eyes, knowing their hard work had paid off—especially the Professor. I had prepared a speech on "life after high school," but my speech became more of a mumble and ramble when it was time to give it. I said things like, "Our mission is not complete—this journey has just begun!" I talked about consequences in life, the love of God and family—things like that. I talked about my parents and I could see them glowing with glee. I thought I saw my dad, that's right. Mr. "Tough Guy," eyes filled up with tears. I mentioned something about my "gift" more metaphorically and my friends knowing what I was kinda talking about, looked at each other.

I could see Herman's eyes looking at Anthony, saying, "I hope that fool don't scare these people talking about his witchcraft!"

Although my speech was a ramble—well, to me—I think I did a good job conveying my message of hope to all the young minds that were present. My parents couldn't have cared less. They were so proud, you would have thought I had just been elected President of the United States.

After my ramble, Principal Dunbar, with help from Ms. Lambert, one of the assistant principals, announced all the graduating class alphabetically. Since I was valedictorian, I was privileged enough to be on stage with the faculty. So, when "Truman" was announced, I proudly shook all the hands that were in the soul train line of diploma excellence and proudly walked back to my seat among the educated elite. My brother, Jeffery, had that oh-shit look on his face because he knew in three years he was expected to be next. After we graduated and everybody got some time with their folks, I met my boys down at the local diner, Yummy's, and got a booth.

Yummy's was a cool place. It was cool because of the owner, Mr. Yang. Mr. Yang came to America as a young boy. Both his parents had died in the Vietnam War, so he was adopted by Colonel Baker.

Although Colonel Baker was a white man, he was everything civil rights.

We didn't know the Colonel; he died before me and my crew were born, therefore leaving his wife to raise Mr. Yang and their other adopted kids. However, his adopted son Yang Po Hung inspired us. We just called him Mr. Yang.

Mr. Yang had eight brothers and sisters and they were all adopted by the Colonel and his wife Carrol, and his rainbow family came from all over the world. They were all smart and educated men and women. Yang was the only one that decided to stay in our small community and open up a place where people, especially young people, could come and hang out, grab a hamburger and just enjoy life.

The coolest thing about Yummy's Diner was that it was established during the early years of segregation when white kids and black kids hung out at different locations. It wasn't that way at Yang's place. I think because Mr. Yang knew segregation destroyed his family and country, he wouldn't allow anything negative at his place.

Mr. Yang knew everyone in our small community and everyone knew him. He started his business by saving his money and not relying on banks that rarely lent money to people of color. Since he paid cash for his place, and green was and is the true color of racism, the powers to be had no problem with Yang's place. He gave such great advice to the young patrons that enjoyed his place that he was almost like a walking fortune cookie. He talked with a deep Asian accent and broken English. We knew he was putting on with the accent because he came to the United States when he was eight. He spoke many languages and I never saw him get mad. In another life he would have been a comedian for sure. He was about 5 feet tall and was a typical Asian, as it related to looks. He never married, but the women loved him. Although he was in his late fifties or early sixties, he was still a good-looking man. At first I thought to myself, but found out later that we all believed, he was fooling around with his main cook, Ms. Thomas, who was a very attractive mid-forties black widow. I guess it was the way she used to call his name and how he would go running like a love sick little puppy. Besides her,

44

all of his other employees were high school kids who wanted to work to earn extra money.

Me and the fellas always got a booth in Yummy's next to the window so we could see people coming. Mr. Yang would sometimes come and sit with us for a few and try to crack jokes. We sat at the booth and reflected on the past, joked about the present and tried to figure out what lay ahead for the future of our close-knit posse. I had a small circle of friends and to this day, over 30 plus years, our friendship has remained close.

Chapter 3

MY POSSE

Posse is a word that was notoriously used when you and a

group of mostly men in the cowboy days together. This posse would

hunt down the perpetrators and if caught, bring them back to the city

and put them on trial—and, no, it wouldn't be a trial like the court

system of today. It would be a trial of public opinion, which always

ended up bad for the perpetrators—normally, in the form of a picnic

hanging. In other words, the patrons of the town would gather their

families, take baskets of food near where the hanging was to take

place and have a picnic—strange, but true. Although, we were long

gone from the days of vigilante justice of the old west, my friends

and I were instrumental in helping one another with getting through

the awkward years of high school and grade school. See, my posse

and I met a long time ago. We met during the times when we were

introduced to each other by the names on our elementary school

desks. My last name was Truman and Herman's last name was

46

Timple, so we sat next to each other. Bruce and Anthony (Amp) sat near the front of the class.

For the most part in the early years, we got along with each other. I think it was during a fight outside between Bruce and some fella, I can't remember his name, that the four of us bonded. Puberty is a strange thing. During the middle school years, one would have assumed that I would be the star athlete, not the nerd that I became. I was about 5 feet 8 inches in the 5th grade. I was one of the biggest kids in our elementary school. My buddies all maxed out about five feet. So when puberty showed its ugly face, I still was 5 feet 8 inches with bumps only a mother could love, while the rest of my posse grew to 6 feet 3 inches, and taller by the time we all entered high school.

What I had going for me was my gift, which I didn't understand and the ability to talk my way out of most things, except when it related to my mom, the Professor. So, as I recall in elementary school, Bruce was in the back of the school and there was this big circle around him and the young man he was getting ready to fight. I remember Herman running in the school and telling me that Bruce was getting ready to fight, I think the guys name was Jacob. That's it, it was Jacob Beasley, the school's bully.

"Hey E, Bruce is outside getting ready to fight Jacob!" Herman was out of breath when he was telling me so it kinda sounded like he was mumbling, but I got the gist of what he was saying.

"Why are they getting ready to fight?"

"I think Jacob pushed him and told him that he was gonna kick his ass at recess!"

Even as a young boy, I thought that was kinda silly, but I remember this kid as trying to be tough. I ran back outside with Herman and sure enough, these two fools were in the middle of a circle with their fists up.

Jacob was doing all the talking. The crowd of kids outside who had formed the fighting circle were talking trying to egg the fight on. Some of the little girls were pleading to Jacob to stop and not to hurt Bruce.

So, when I got there, I just walked in the middle of the ring and started talking to Jacob. With both hands on my knees from being

48

tired of running back outside with Herman, I politely assumed the bended knee position next to Jacob. "Jacob—what are you getting ready to do dude?"

"E—this ain't about you."

The funny thing about being the biggest kid at the school was that no one messed with you. Even if they didn't know anything about you, they wouldn't mess with you. But, since I was the biggest kid in the school and my dad was legendary—everyone knew what dad had done to a few gang members—Jacob probably assumed that I was not only big but also tough like my dad. Jacob was afraid of me.

Out of breath, I said, "Man—you must not know what's getting ready to happen to you, dude."

"What you mean by that—I don't have anything against you E. It's just this motherfucker here." For some reason, kids thought cursing made you tough and I guess they must have thought it made them seem cool.

When I started talking to Jacob, Bruce relaxed his hands down near his sides and started listening to our conversation. It still was about ten minutes before our recess came to an end, so the crowd grew. The funny thing is that I can't recall any of the teachers around before the fight night—or fight day. Looking up at Jacob still with my hands on my knees, I said, "Boy, I wouldn't do that." Jacob relented a little because he first thought I was talking about jumping in the fight if it got started, but I knew better.

I wasn't a fighter—hell, I was just smart with a gift from God that I didn't understand at the time. I asked Jacob, "Do you remember the kid that got beat really bad at Dyers Park about a year ago—I know you got to remember because everyone was talking about it."

"Yeah—I remember."

Although Bruce was listening to our conversation, he couldn't make out everything I was saying. I stood up and whispered something in Jacob's right ear. When I finished Jacob said, "Man— Bruce, I was just playing with you. I don't want to fight you—why everybody out here thinking that there is going to be a fight. Me and Bruce is cool—we were just playing with y'all fools and y'all went for it." Some of the kids walked away laughing. Some were shaking their heads like they just missed the fight of the century, but more importantly, there was no fight that day. Jacob walked over to Bruce.

Bruce still was a little confused, but Jacob started laughing. "Boy—we really had them going."

"Aww, aww, yeah, we sure did." Jacob held his hand out for Bruce to shake it and Bruce shook it—they both burst out with laughter.

"Man, what did you say to him?" Even though the fellas would ask, it would be years before I would tell them what I said that shook Jacob.

Throughout this whole ordeal, two things stood out as I looked through the sea of excited kids waiting on a fight. One, Herman was standing by my side as if to say, I got your back if someone else tries to jump in the fight and two, Amp was rapping and trying to console the crying girls who were at the fighting circle to witness what they thought was going to be a lashing by Jacob. The way he was doing it is what I remember. We still talk about those awkward elementary school years today. Now they rag me because compared to them as grown men from high school to adulthood, I haven't grown much.

My posse was my family, my brothers. They were just as close to me as my biological family were. Herman Timple was a hyper, smart athlete who was raised by his grandmother. He spent a lot of time at home because his grand mom, Ms. Nadene, had Alzheimer's at an early age. Alzheimer's was one of those diseases that, during the time of our youth, there wasn't much information on. We just assumed Ms. Nadene was sick, or crazy. Herman had to grow up fast, but he never complained about his situation. He was probably at my place and I was at his place more than my other two friends.

Herman was about 6' 5" and weigh about 220 pounds. He had blazing speed. I think he ran the 40 yard dash in about 4.03 seconds. Like my other friends who were highly touted by colleges around the world, he could have played any sport in college.

Like Herman, Bruce and Amp were unbelievable athletes. Both guys stood over 6'3" and both were highly touted as athletes. However, Amp would be the athlete who would go on to have a stellar career in the National Football League. Amp played linebacker (9 pro bowls).

I used to love going to his games just to see how many girls I could be introduced to. I used to lie to the ladies at the NFL games and say I played high school ball with Amp, but they would always know right away I was lying. The fellas would hear me, look at each other, and just shake their heads.

These three guys were my best friends and I could tell you many stories that would capture the true essence of our friendship, but that's for another story.

It became tradition for us to get together after the game. Bruce was already with Amp, so me and Herman would either drive, or fly to where his team was playing.

We wouldn't go out with the other NFL football players. We would find a local place similar to Mr. Yang's place, get a booth and reflect on life like we did in the old days. Herman, after a pretty stellar football career in college, and because of several knee injuries, decided not to pursue a professional football career like Amp. Truthfully, he was a better football player than Amp. Herman moved to Washington and has been working for the government since college. He swears he has an important job. I told him he ain't nothing but an over paid janitor.

Then there's Bruce. Bruce ran track, played football and could have played both football and basketball in college if he had enough time—he chose football. When he graduated from college, he went to graduate school where he got his MBA. I always thought Bruce was kinda slow, but I guess you can't judge a book by its cover. Bruce and Amp were closer than the rest of the crew, so when Amp asked Bruce to come with him to run his affairs, Bruce did just that. Bruce did a great job with Amp's money. While Amp was playing, Bruce established several lucrative businesses. I think their net worth was about thirty million dollars. My friends were all tall, athletic, and smart. I was the only shrimp in the bunch.

We called Bruce "Pretty-Boy" and man he hated it. Well, the ladies loved Bruce. Not only was he tall, but he had looks to go with his demanding athletic model like figure. His complexion wasn't too light, or too dark, but as the women would say, was just right. He had the jet-black fine hair and perfect teeth. He wasn't a ladies man, or a person that dated a lot. He dated the same girl all the way from high school to college. He would eventually marry his high school

sweet heart.

I always and still to this day tease Bruce and Amp. I would tell

Bruce, I thought he was gonna put Amp into the poor house.

"Amp—you know Bruce is spending your money on nothing but

drugs and prostitutes."

"Naw —he's been doing pretty good wit it."

"Awe, EJ, you just jealous—if you wasn't magical, or had those

voodoo powers, you wouldn't have even graduated from high

school."

We would rip on each other and laugh like this for hours.

These guys have always had my back, and I have always had

theirs. When I was being harassed in high school by bullies, my

friends would always be there to make things right—even fighting,

or getting kicked out of school for a day or two. They knew how my

parents were and they didn't want me to get in trouble. But most of

the time, once someone knew who I hung out with, they backed off.

In exchange, my friends knew if they needed my help with school

projects, I would always be there for them. I was very persistent with making sure my posse had everything they needed to be successful in school. In fact, they all did well in school, even Bruce with his math—which I proudly take credit for.

Poor Bruce, I can remember him having a hard time with math. He needed the math class not only to graduate, but if he didn't pass math, he would have lost his football scholarship, or he would have to go to summer school before he could go to school.

"What up, Bruce?"

"Man, I don't know," he would say in a not so Bruce voice.

If you would have known or met Bruce, you would have known he was the type of person that was always upbeat. So it was kinda strange to see him looking like he had just lost a family member.

"C'mon dude, you my boy and I know you." I would jokingly say. "Don't make me use my gift," I would continue, while whistling Twilight Zone music, trying to make him laugh, to no avail.

"Yo, EJ, if I don't pass math this quarter, not only will I not graduate, but I will lose my scholarship." He was devastated.

"Well, we can't let that happen." I rounded up the posse. "Yo—fellas, we got a mission. Bruce is failing math and we need to help him."

Amp would joke about the situation. "Man we all know Bruce is an idiot."

"Come on Amp, that shit's not funny. You know he needs our help."

"I know man, you know I had to rag on him."

"What's the plan?"

"Hell E—you are the smartest motherfucker in the school, not including that magic shit you got going for you—what in the hell do you think our dumb asses is going to help you with?"

"Yeah, E, Amp is right."

"Two dumbasses leading one dumbass." They would just laugh at what they were saying.

"C'mon, guys."

"A'ight E."

"What's the plan?"

"Well, we got eight weeks to get dumbass—just kidding," (everyone erupted into laughter) "ready for his final math exam. We are going to have to meet at my house every Saturday and drill him until he gets it."

"WHAT!"

"Every Saturday!"

"I don't know about that, E."

"Amp, what don't you know—it ain't like you got a date or something, and you should be tired of taking your cousin out to the pizza house every Saturday."

Through everyone's laughter he replied, "Fuck you, Herman!"

Through it all, we met every Saturday like clockwork at my house for eight weeks. Some things Bruce would get, and some things would take reinforcement; eventually, he got all of it. Bruce passed math with a C. The boys and I liked to kid with him and tell him that his C grade belonged to us.

That's the way it was with my friends and me. We loved each other. If someone was sick, we were there. If someone lost a loved one, we were there. In the city of Bridgeport, West Virginia, that's how people lived and treated each other. Yeah, racial discrimination and tension was, and still is, part of the culture in which we grew up, but it didn't define most of the people who lived in what I thought to be a majestic place.

My father died around the time Amp was in his 4th year of professional football. He had an important game on the same day of my father's funeral. There's nothing more revealing and honoring when you look up in a crowd during a time of sorrow and you see not only the people you knew would be there, but also the people who you knew had other obligations and although they wanted to be there, they couldn't make it. All the fellows made it to my father's funeral. What really made me proud was Amp made it when he knew he had something important to do—an important game.

Amp, who just got off of a chartered plane, walked in the church, knelt down in front of my mom with tears in his eyes and said, " Ms. Renee, I loved your husband, he—he--he was the only dad that I knew." I knew he was reflecting back to all the candy, football games, praise, and positive reinforcement my dad would give him. He embraced my mom and cried like a baby. I never saw my friend

59

cry, or even sad. I learned later from Bruce because Amp missed the play-off game they lost, he was fined fifty thousand dollars and suspended for two games the next season. Amp never mentioned it to me.

Amp was one of the guys you would have thought had all the answers as to how to pick up women. Even though he was this great athlete, we--the fellas and I--thought he was trying to be a ladies' man. This goes all the way back to when we all bonded in elementary school. I still can see him going up to the young ladies, trying to console them because one of our friends was about to fight. What I finally realized was that Amp wasn't trying to be a ladies man. However, this was the way he treated all women because he was raised by women and seven sisters. His mother, whom I thought was the best cook in the world and one of the nicest women on the planet, raised him and his seven sisters in a house that was about four doors from my house. Amp was the baby, and his sisters treated him like one.

So, Amp had the goods on how to console and treat women. What I realize is not that he wasn't trying to be a ladies' man, rapping to any and every women he ran across—it was that he showed ultimate deference for ALL women. That's why it was special when he came to my dad's funeral and when he embraced my mom. That was the most emotional thing I had ever seen—you would have thought that my mom was his mom.

"E, I told Amp you would understand if he couldn't make it to the funeral and I would represent the both of us. Man E, Amp looked at me like I was a traitor." He said, "E is our friend and brother. His mom and dad are like our parents; the Super Bowl couldn't keep me away from this funeral."

My friends are real—my Friends are my family, my brothers from another mother—my posse.

Chapter 4

THE GIFT

Even at an early age, I had the "Gift." My mom told me I was one of God's angels. Dad would just look at me and say, "Boy, I don't care what type of powers you think you got from heaven, while your butt is here on earth, living with me, I got the ok from the boss up-stairs to beat that ass if you get out of hand."

I was always able to predict certain things were going to happen before they happened. My friends use to always tell me in a joking way the only reason they were my friends were because they wanted their future kept anonymous.

My friends thought my gift was cool. Herman used to say, "Man, E, you would think with your special visions you would be able to see those ass whippings these fools at school was trying to administer to you daily." When Herman said that, we all just burst out laughing uncontrollably.

I would just say, "Man, I know y'all got my back."

As I got older, my skills—mom would call them visions—became more poignant. At first I was scared, but as I got older, fear turned into frustration and later became acceptance. I figured if God entrusted me with an ability to see in the future he must have needed help with all the millions of requests he got on a daily basis.

As my visions became more poignant, so did my gift. Oh—I still had the gift of vision, but now God in all of his wisdom felt I needed all the powers of an angel. I was kind of a visual angel on earth. I mean, God gave me the power to grant wishes. No, I couldn't grant wishes for money or influence. I couldn't rid the world from poverty, hunger, or incurable diseases. However, God gave me the gift and I knew if given to the right person, it could make a change so drastic and devastating, it would transform their life forever.

Now, we all know if God wanted to, he could change the world and make it any way he wanted. But remember, he gave man the greatest gift—the gift of free thought, free will, and he wasn't about to interfere with that. God knew there would always be special times when he needed to project his power of persuasion on someone to help someone else that was in his favor. That's where I came in. I was God's go-to man, a sort of middleman to be called on from time to time. My job was helping one of his fallen children realize their love for him.

Around the time I had settled into my new job after post-graduate as a Professor of History at Vanderbilt University, God was calling on me to use my gift, and I was listening.

Chapter 5

THE ORDER—SINS OF THE FATHER

Larry "Bubba" Dixon was a bright and intelligent incoming freshman at Silicon High. People say Silicon High was named after John Silicon. They believe John Silicon, who was a high-ranking officer in the Confederate Army, started the KKK in Pulaski, Tennessee, with some of his Confederate cohorts. It was John Silicon who came up with using the Greek word Kuklos, which means "Circle of Brothers." As he would put it, "If we don't save our country from those fucking Lincoln bastards, the niggers and the Jews will take over—hell, one of those black, uppity, spear-chuckers might even try to become president. We might have lost the war, but if I got something to do with it, we ain't gonna lose our country." I guess ole Silicon must be turning over in his grave, because in 2008, the Senator from Chicago, a black man, Barrack Obama, my classmate, went on to become the 44th President of the United States.

Larry grew up in McCormick, South Carolina. The interesting thing about McCormick is, that while it's only 70 miles from the capital of South Carolina, Columbia, by 21st century standards is considered one of the most racist and backward thinking cities in the United States. The blacks in McCormick lived across the railroad tracks from the whites. These living conditions are traditional throughout the United States—black people living across the railroad tracks from white people has always been a sort of a condition for white people to consider themselves safe from the people that they repress. Although South Carolina is making some strides in changing racial injustice, McCormick still has a long way to go. The upper-state blacks jokingly would say, "Boy do you know Jim Crow still exists in McCormick?" However, their joke wasn't far from reality. The saying for people who have had the great opportunity to deal with the McCormick judicial system was, "Don't get caught in McCormick!" It was always baffling to outsiders that most African-Americans who left McCormick seemed like they just got out of a concentration camp, or as if they had just been freed from slavery. I grew up in a town in West Virginia that wasn't much different from

McCormick; the town had a high percentage of African-Americans. However, the small town was controlled by just a few white rich families.

McCormick has a population of 10,233—48 percent white, 49 percent black and a poverty rate of 20. McCormick has a black sheriff and most of its police force is African-American. However, the "New Order" controls McCormick. The Order is an established organization headed by white businessmen and political leaders who set the agenda for the city of McCormick. Most of these businessmen and political leaders grew up in the KKK with their fathers and grandfathers being Klan members.

The New Order understood times were changing and the only way to combat the niggers from oppressing white people was to have power and influence in the business and political spectrum. Larry's father, Billy Ray, knew this all too well. Billy Ray Clemson Dixon was a prominent businessman, not only in McCormick, but also throughout South Carolina. He owned one of the biggest and influential corporations in the world—The OTOCH Corporation. Billy Ray also was a wolf in sheep's clothing.

In other words, he knew how to deal with the nigger problem.

Billy Ray was about 5 feet tall and just as round. He was pale, with thin lips and a thin sharp nose. He had small hands and large feet. Everyone used to say he looked like the penguin on the 1960s Batman show.

On the surface, Billy Ray seemed pleasant. He was smart, had great orator skills, and always made everyone feel accepted. However, Billy Ray knew how to deal with black people—hell, most of his employees were black. He dealt with what they called the "nigger problem," not in the old traditional way of making them feel unwanted, but in a new and special way of making them feel accepted.

Billy Ray took a chapter right out of the writings of Willie Lynch and kept black people in check by keeping them divided among themselves. He knew although McCormick was about 49 percent black, most of the blacks that lived in McCormick were uneducated. And if they were educated, they justified the unjust behavior from white people with a "You know—that's how it is here" type of attitude. When Billy Ray and the rest of the Order would convene, he made sure they understood the new dynamics of controlling their problem, and it couldn't be done in the open with ropes and whips. He knew the ropes and whips had to be replaced with division, labor, and economic discord. He would always say black people were our biggest commodity.

With this ideology, Billy Ray ran his business with division, deception, and a nice toping of religion. He would always tell his Order members that, "If we keep the niggers divided and fighting among themselves—make them think we are on their side when something happens or goes wrong, and always paint a picture of Christian Faith in how we live our lives—they will always, and I mean always, think we have their best interest."

Larry grew up in this racist environment and learned everything from his poppa, as he would call him. Larry adored his parents, but worshiped his dad. Besides God, there was no one on this earth Larry held in a higher regard. Larry knew South Carolina and all states in the U.S. have since outlawed lynching, and the days of Jim Crow were sort of a thing of the past. He enjoyed going with his dad over to grandpas. Grandpa use to talk about his father and some of

69

the things he did to niggers when they got sassy. Listening to his

grandpa, Larry would sometimes wish he could have been there

helping out his great-grandfather during the days of what he thought

of as "Nigger disobedience." Larry's vitriol was toxic and the hatred

he had against African-Americans was unmatched. Larry stayed

patient, because he knew the New Order would introduce him to a

new type of oppression, Economic Racism.

Every now and then, there would be a mysterious type of

homicide that would occur in McCormick. Most of the blacks in

town suspected Klan play and that it was initiated by the Order, but

they couldn't prove it. Even when the Sheriff would try to

investigate one of the mystery murders he was shut down by the

Order. Larry spent most of his school years learning the way of the

Order. He also became a big fan of the Turner Diaries. The Turner

Diaries is a 1978 novel by William Luther Pierce, founder of the

White Nationalist Organization National Alliance, published under

the pseudonym "Andrew Macdonald." This novel depicts a violent

revolution in the United States which leads to the overthrow of the

federal government, nuclear war, and ultimately, a race war.

Larry was driven by hate because that's all he knew. You would think in the 21st century a young man with his intellect would be more aware of how diverse the world has become. You would think a brilliant young man like Larry wouldn't have such tunnel vision. However, Larry loved his father and wanted to impress him by living up to his father's twisted ideology of the worldview.

Larry excelled in school and learned what he would call "the devil's doctrine." He thought in order to have the upper hand he needed to learn what the enemy was talking about. He believed blacks shouldn't have the same rights as whites. He always told his friends he wished he lived during slavery and that the Jim Crow era was weak on niggers. Larry hated blacks, not because they did anything to him, but because he was keen on believing the government was giving blacks rights and things they didn't deserve.

Like all Klansmen, Larry believed the Constitution was flawed and "The only good nigger, is a dead nigger." His dad would later teach him a good nigger was a working nigger and that nigger need to be working for you. He studied old history and believed William Luther Pierce and Willie Lynch were gods. In 2007, Larry Bubba

Dixon graduated with his class of 200 and was headed to Vanderbilt University to pursue an education in History.

Larry's cell rang to the sounds of the country group, Sugarland. On occasions, he would change the ring tone on his cell. He had a country song for every number he had in his cell.

"Hey, baby!"

"Hey Lar'—what you doin?"

"Nothing. Just sitting around thinking about school and things."

"What about?"

"Well, did I ever tell you why I chose Vandy?"

"No."

"Well, I chose Vandy because if I wanted to go to a good school, I best be going to a school in the south."

"Why?"

"I figured, all those liberal schools up north would be infested with uneducated black people—you know the 'affirm folks.'"

That's what Larry called African-Americans who were in college or had graduated from college. He believed all African-Americans were in school because of affirmative action. "And I ain't got time to be learning all of that jig-a-boo bullshit. Shit baby, If I'm gonna go to college, I at least want to be around mostly my kind and taught by my kind."

"Oh—I see."

Larry would try to be a little politically correct in how he talked about African-Americans around his girlfriend Susan Fredman (he called her Sue) because she didn't see life as radically and as distorted as Larry did, though she sympathized with his views.

"Are we seeing each other later?"

"Yeah. Where you want to go?"

"I don't care—what about Sonics?"

"That's cool."

"Okay, baby, I'll see you around eight."

"O.K. Love you."

"Love you too."

When Larry was with his crew, however, he would express another viewpoint. Larry's favorite thing to say was, "It'll be a cold day in hell before I let a nigger teach me—maybe they can teach me

how to run and jump like a monkey." His boys would just laugh.

He went on boasting. "Y'all know I chose Vandy so I can learn

history from southern white people. Niggers don't teach history; they

don't even know where they come from. Maybe they can teach

nigger history at Martin Luther Koon High, but not real history."

Larry's views were so distorted.

Billy Ray was a little upset Larry decided to leave McCormick.

He always wanted Larry to stay home and maybe run his businesses

when he retired. However, that was not to happen. Although Larry

loved his father, he wanted to see other places and do different

things. He didn't care about seeing all the wonderful sights that

America or any other country had to offer; he just wanted to see and

visit some of the places that his confederate heroes like General Lee,

Baldwin of Spartanburg, and Lt. Colonel Bee of Charleston, South

Carolina fought during the Civil War. Larry knew this would be a

hard sell to his dad, but he knew four things. First, he knew he loved

his poppa. Second, he knew he didn't want to run his daddy's

businesses. Third, he knew he wanted to go to college; and fourth, he knew he had a secret about his daddy only he, his daddy and God knew.

Larry and Billy Ray always bumped heads when it came to Larry's future. "Hey, Bubba, when you finish dicking around with your boys, come home. I need to talk with you."

In a long and drawled out voice, almost whinny tone, Larry responded, "Yes, sir." He knew all too well what his poppa wanted to talk to him about. Larry tried to sound up beat when he saw his dad sitting in the study.

"What's up Poppa?"

"Hey, son!" he said with excitement. "Have you thought about what we discussed about your future?"

"Oh—uh—yes, sir."

"Well?"

"Well, dad, I know how you wanted me to stay in McCormick and run your businesses, but I really want to attend college. You told me you weren't planning on retiring for another 15 years and I thought I would attend college and have something to bring to the table when I finish."

Larry was pleading his case like a seasoned lawyer, as if he was trying to keep his client from getting the death penalty.

With a stern look and calm voice Billy Ray asked Larry, "Well, son, what type of degree are you wanting to seek? Your mother subtly mentioned that you applied and was accepted in to Vandy. Vandy is a good school, I wish I attended school there. I heard they had a great business department—one of the best in the south."

Larry looked at his father as if he already gotten the permission he wanted to study history and was trying to be a wise ass.
In the manliest voice he could muster, Larry told his dad, "Dad—I want to study HISTORY!"

His dad burst into laughter. But, Billy Ray's laughter quickly turned to anger.

"How in the HELL you think a history degree is going to help you with running the family businesses?"

Larry thought, "How in the HELL do you manage to run a successful business without any degree?" but he knew better than to say that. Larry knew this was a set up and he really didn't have an answer for his dad.

"Son, you are not going to Vanderbilt University! The decision is final!"

Larry loved his father, but he knew he wanted to attend college and he was going to, no matter what decision his dad thought he had made for him. Larry looked his dad straight in the eyes and said, "I GOT A SECRET!" and left the room.

Chapter 6

ANOTHER PROFESSOR

I finished my undergraduate degree in three years from

Harvard. I continued with my graduate degree at my Alma Mater.

After I graduated from grad school, I applied and was accepted at,

you guessed it, Harvard University, where I earned a PhD in History.

In the spring of 1987, I was just starting my new job. I laughed to

myself, thinking, "Look at me—a big time Negro professor at an

elite university in the south. I wouldn't have thought in a million

years I would be a professor here at Vanderbilt!"

I knew the history of most universities in the south and where

they stood with African-American faculty tenure and it wasn't good.

Hell, one of the most liberal schools in the country, my Alma Mater,

didn't start accepting blacks until a little before the civil rights

movement.

Freddie Gavin

When I started at Vanderbilt, there was only one black person who had been there longer than me, Mr. Bailey. John Bailey was a tall, thin man who knew everybody at the university. Some of the staff jokingly told me he had been janitor at the university about the time they opened their doors in the 1800s. Mr. Bailey was a quiet and pleasant man. Even though times had changed, he still responded to everyone, from students to faculty with, "Yes ma'am," or "No, sir." Mr. Bailey was a special person to me because he said little and observed everything. As time went by, Mr. Bailey and I developed a father and son type of relationship. It wasn't driven by simple pleasantries he received or gave to the students or other faculty members, it was driven by faith, love, deference and the idea that I was one of a few black men teaching at a southern university.

John Rufus Bailey was more than a janitor and knew racism all too well. You see, all though Mr. Bailey was aging and had out lived most of his family members, he was still sharp. At the time I met Mr. Bailey he was in his early 70s and had been working at the university since his discharge from the war. What made Mr. Bailey special was his resolve. Mr. Bailey would never marry and raise a

79

family, because as he once told me, "It wasn't time for me to bring a child, or have a wife in a world that treated me as if I was chattel."

He would always say, "Son, dignity is a wonderful thing if they would allow you to have some." I kinda knew what he meant. Mr. Bailey was a very smart man and he would always talk to me like Jesus was talking to his disciples—he used many parables. Mr. Bailey was trying to convey to me that in America, a black man couldn't really be a whole man. Yes, he would be able to fight for his country, eventually play sports and engage in politics with other white men, he may even be able to tenure at a university; but there was one thing that separated them from us that we would never overcome—the denial of dignity. He reminded me that no matter how much his father tried to just be a man, there was always some hate-filled white person ready to bring him down, especially when he was with his family. He saw his father, a strong man, denigrated many times and it broke him.

Mr. Bailey saw the man he looked up to disrespected in a way that was hard for him to explain and decided a long time ago that although he longed for a family and a son to carry his name, he knew he didn't want a family in a time where even his name wasn't truly his name. I understood what Mr. Bailey was talking about when he said dignity was all a man wanted in life. With dignity, you can raise a family, protect them without controversy, and provide them with the same things in life most white people in America take for granted.

The university was fond of Mr. Bailey. But there were things the university didn't know about this great man. What the university didn't know about Mr. Bailey was he was a Tuskegee University graduate and Airman with eight kills and that he left with a dishonorable discharge. Mr. Bailey's discharge all came as a result of his heroism while on leave visiting his parents in South Georgia. The university didn't know his heroism came from striking a white enlisted soldier who was attempting to rape and kill a black female and her infant son. The only thing happened to the enlisted soldier was he was moved to another state. Mr. Bailey's only option was to be discharged from the service, never go back to Georgia, and move to another state, or country to start a new life.

I knew Mr. Bailey because he reminded me of my father. He would always make a point every day to come by my office and in the sweetest voice ask me, "EJ, how are you doing?" To my students and most faculty members, I was either Professor, or Professor Eric—but to Mr. Bailey, I was son, Eric, or EJ. Because of my dad's death, I revered him as a father figure. He heard everything that was going on around the campus and when things were favorable to me, he told me. Even when things were not so favorable to me, he told me.

Recently, he overheard some of the brass talking about improving on minority enrollment. He also heard them discussing about hiring another African-American to jump-start a program specified in the study of the African-American race as a whole. This person was to head the whole department. I thought, "WOW! Vandy is stepping up its game!" He heard the name Eric Dyson, but since he was a lot older and his hearing was a little impaired, he thought he heard Patrick Nixon.

I knew Vanderbilt, like most southern universities, was looking for what they called a 'System Negro.' A System Negro was just

82

another racial understated name for "control." The Negro Vanderbilt wanted was the Clarence Thomas type. The kind that would use the system, like affirmative action, and once he was given an opportunity to move up in the hierarchy of white passage, he would forget who, or where he came from. The type of Negro that believed in some strange way he was one of them. The type of Negro that didn't mind marrying a white woman—not that there was anything wrong with marrying a person from another race, but the idea that if I consider myself one of them, then I must also be like them in all facets of life, even marriage. Vanderbilt wanted to hire another black person but it had to be one they could control. I knew in the practical sense I wasn't the type of Negro they were looking for, but I guess it must have been something I said in the interview process that made them smitten with me. I didn't have any problem with the way Vanderbilt's white establishment wanted to control me because I knew the only person had control over my destiny was me. I knew the reasoning behind accepting tenure at Vanderbilt wasn't about trying to move up in the world of crony capitalism, or even about me, but my tenure here was driven by my gift, which was appointed by a higher power.

Michael Eric Dyson, a brilliant African-American scholar, decided not to work at Vandy. His rational couldn't be more profound. He knew among the brass there was skepticism and controversy surrounding his visit. However, they knew Professor Dyson was by far one of the most brilliant minds since W.E.B Du Bois. Although the Vanderbilt faculty recommended him unanimously, the Vanderbilt dean refused to make the appointment. In his remarks to a local Tennessee newspaper Professor Dyson said, "I'm sure that philosophically and theoretically Vanderbilt is quite riveted to increasing and expanding the number of minority faculty, but philosophy and practice are two different things."

I have been at Vanderbilt now as a professor for the last 22 years and I have noticed some mild advancement with the way African-Americans are treated. Not since Joseph Johnson has there been a push to promote more of a diverse culture at Vanderbilt; but change is always slow. I have had a great career here at the university and have been offered several positions since my stay, but I'm fine where I am. I figure I'll be like old man Bailey. I'll keep it simple.

I will continue to do my job—seen but slightly heard—and always

ready to educate young minds that have a passion for history.

Chapter 7

A DIRTY LITTLE SECRET

Penny Johnson, or PJ, was a very beautiful African-American

woman. She attended Silicon High school during the same time

Bubba's oldest sister Marie attended. I think they might have been

the same age. Penny lived with her mother Valarie Thompson and

stepfather, Tyrone "Tank" Thompson.

Everybody knew Tank. Tank was considered one of the best

football players in the state of South Carolina. He was a little older

than Valarie, and everybody wanted to play football like Tank. In

fact, I remember reading articles on this next O.J. Simpson type god

of a football player from South Carolina. There were even rumors

kids who knew Tank would fight over who was going to be him

when they engaged in sandlot football, even many of the white kids.

Tank was like the Michael Jordan of football, but he wasn't as

recognized as Mike, and he was a little before Sir Airiness. Amp

read about the football star that never was and loved Tank so much he wore his football number in high school, college and even when he was playing professional football. He wanted to one day meet his idol, which he would eventually do.

Tank played during the early 50s right at the time college coaches were looking for what they knew was going to change their football programs forever—a Negro. Even the legendary and racist Bear Bryant who claimed he would never recruit a black player came to McCormick high school to recruit Tank. Tank didn't give a fuck about playing college football, or professional football. Like he would say, "Man, fuck those redneck mother fuckers! Shit we are just a few years removed from slavery and these bastards think we can be auctioned by the biggest bidder. If I'm gonna play football, I'm gonna play for black people wit' black people."

I was told Tank told Bear to kiss his ass. I think Bear called him a boy and he didn't like that. If you know Tank, you would know that no one messed with him—a real live Leroy Brown. Not like my dad, but most people think that Jim Croce song, Leroy Brown, was actually written about Tank. Not that he was a bad guy, but he took shit from no one; and I mean no one. He had a calmness and coolness that drove most people crazy, especially white folks. They didn't know how to take him, but they knew not to fuck with him. Even the Order stayed clear. Not that he was above reproach, he was just one of those guys that would die for what he believed and it didn't matter the culprit, i.e., New Order, Old Order, or any Order. He has since calmed down his feelings towards white people, but he still didn't have a lot of trust of them and he definitely didn't take any shit, from them or anyone.

I think Val and the kids made Tank a more tolerable person. He was part of the teamsters—the old teamsters. Tank drove trucks for a living. He eventually bought his own rig; a big milestone for a black guy, especially from McCormick. Although Tank was this God of a football player, Penny could always tell Tank was really a big softy. From my understanding, I think Amp told me Tank didn't even watch sports on T.V. Hell, Tank cared more about Valarie, her kids, fishing and hunting than sports.

Amp said he met his idol his third year in the league. He said the meeting was happenstance and when he met Tank, he really seemed taken aback someone from the NFL had recognized his talent from the past and honored him even when he never played

beyond high school. Tank appreciated Amp's admiration for him

and they would become friends over the years. Tank even came to a

few games as Amp's guest. I also knew, even though Amp didn't

tell me, that he bought Tank a brand new rig for his trucking

business to replace the old one.

McCormick had many secrets. With so many mysterious,

unsolved deaths one would think McCormick was the place to

commit murder. Everyone used to joke, "If you wanted to get away

with murder, bury the remains in McCormick." They'd also joke

that the reason why the government never found Jimmy Hoffa was

because he was murdered and buried in McCormick. I think Tank

thought that was true, but realistically speaking, Hoffa may not have

been buried there. I would bet my life a lot of people the Order was

displeased with were.

Penny knew Tank wasn't her father. Although she loved Tank,

she would always ask her mother about the whereabouts of her

biological dad. And like a broken record Val would tell her, "Your

dad was a fling I had one summer with a solider from Fort Gordon."

And when she would ask if her mother ever heard from him, she would say, "Baby, I'm married to a wonderful man—and you know he loves you; just as much, or even more than he loves your sisters and brothers. I don't spend my time wondering about a dead beat. I tell you what—when you locate him, tell that bastard he owes me thirty thousand dollars in child support."

"MOM! You know I just want to at least know who he was."

"Well baby—I don't know how to get in touch with him. I think he's from New York. Baby—maybe one day, when you graduate from high school and go on to college, you can locate him."

In a sort of a despairing voice Penny replied, "Alright, mom."

Val knew she wasn't being up front with her daughter. Even the love of her life, Tank, didn't know who the father of her child was, but he didn't care. There were only four people who knew the truth about her father—God, her father, Val, and Bubba—and none of them were talking.

Although Billy Ray was a successful businessman and was now the leader of one of the most influential cults since the famous Skulls and Bones, he had a problem—drinking. One of the rules of the

New Order was to be light in drink. In other words, don't be a drunken fool. One night Billy Ray was coming home from a drinking binge when he saw Valarie walking home from a night out with friends. Billy Ray saw Valarie and pulled over. In his southern and drunken voice Billy said, "Hey, Miss Johnson, do you need a ride?"

With her head down, she politely said, "No, thank you, sir." Valarie's dad worked many years for Billy Ray and Valarie knew her dad relied on his employment to support their family.

In a kinda slurred voice Billy Ray said, "How about you get your little butt in this vehicle so I can take you home? I know Clarence don't want his little angel out here at night by herself."

Reluctantly, Valarie got in his car.

When Valarie got into Billy Ray's car, he reached over on her side of the vehicle and assisted in closing the door. She could smell the alcohol on his breath and clothes. Although Valarie was a little reluctant, she really wasn't afraid of Mr. Dixon. Why should she be? He was always nice to her and her family. Her dad had worked for him for a billion years and was always respectful to her mom.

91

"Mr. Dixon, I think you missed my turn." Billy Ray passed right by the railroad tracks that lead to Valarie's house. "Mr. Dixon, I think you just passed my house."

"Shut up bitch! I heard you the first time."

Valarie became very nervous and scared. Billy Ray turned off Old Piedmont Road. Piedmont road wasn't used much. It used to be a hot spot for all the white kids on Saturday night, but some of the old blacks use to think it was a place where they held Klan meetings. It was now vacant land owned by the Dixons.

"Alright Little Val—that's what your little nigger friends call you, right?"

"Yes, sir."

"Get your ass out of my car!"

Valarie got out of Billy Ray's car and started nervously shaking. Billy Ray approached her from the driver's side and without saying a word, slapped her. She fell to the ground but didn't say a word. "I heard all you black bitches had good pussy and love to fuck—is that true?"

Whimpering, she said "Nooooo, sir."

92

That angered Billy Ray, so when Valarie said no, he slapped her again. He asked her again, "DO ALL BLACK BITCHES LIKE YOU WHO ROAM THE STREETS AT NIGHT LOVE TO FUCK?"

She eventually caught on and said, "Yes, sir."

Billy Ray ordered Valarie to pull off her dress and underwear and he began to violently rape her over and over for more than an hour. Valarie could smell the alcohol on Billy Ray. The only thing she could think about was, "How did I get myself in this situation?" She knew she had to survive, so she kept quiet and followed all of Billy Ray's instructions. When he finished raping her, he told her to put back on her underwear and dress. He also told her if she told anyone he would fire her dad and have him arrested for stealing from him.

When Billy Ray dropped Valarie home, he had the audacity to go with her to the door. Valarie's dad came to the door as Valarie was coming in the door. "Gurl, where in the hell have you been?"

Before she could speak, Billy Ray spoke for her. "Now, come on, Clarence—it's not her fault she was late. I saw her up the road a spell, I guess she was coming home from friends. I saw a few ignorant white kids pushing her around a little. That's when I stopped the small excursion and told Valarie she better let me take her home. Clarence –you know how these crazy ass white kids can be."

"Thanks Mr. Dixon—I really appreciate what you did for my little girl."

If Mr. Johnson really knew what had happened to his little girl he would have tried to kill Billy Ray, which would have certainly caused a serious race riot.

Before Clarence went to bed, he went by his daughter's room, which she shared with her two sisters and apologized for his anger. Valarie was in the bathroom with the door closed, crying and in shock. Clarence called out her name by her bedroom door and she answered in a timid and frightened voice, "Daddy, I'm in here!"

"Baby, you know I love you right."

"Yes sir."

"Well—I wanted to apologize for my behavior tonight and I promise to trust you a little more; O.K. sweetie?"

"Okay daddy." He said and went to bed.

Penny Angel Johnson was born December 25th, 1992.

Everybody was so happy for Valarie. Although Mr. Johnson was upset his oldest daughter had conceived a baby at such a young age, he welcomed little Penny with open arms. Little Penny was beautiful, bubbly and had her daddy's eyes. Abortions were not an option in a Christian household like the Johnsons. And even if abortions were common, Mr. Johnson wouldn't have allowed it. Valarie's conception of little Penny was looked upon as a gift from God in our community, especially being born on Christmas. In the white community, Penny's birth was looked as just another uneducated mixed-nigger to help vitalize their community with labor when she became old enough to work.

Chapter 8

A LOVE LETTER FROM WILLIE LYNCH

On the banks of the James River in the colony of Virginia,

Willie Lynch delivered his famous How to Letter 1712. The Willie

Lynch Letter: "The Making Of A Slave!" speech to a crowd of a few

hundred slave-owners. Just like the famous "Idiot Books", Willie

gave a riveting detailed speech in manual style on how to fix the

slave owners problem of nigger disobedience. This speech was so

vital that his methods are still used now in the 21st century. Even

Willie's last name has become a word that can be found in Webster's

dictionary. Lynch means to kill by mob action, without lawful trial,

as by hanging. So, the significance of Willie's speech on that bright

sunny day has been a sort of Constitution of the United States for

controlling the Negro.

Willie's speech started out like most speeches with greetings and

ending with thanks. His speech even chastised the slave owner for

using primitive methods, such as hanging. He expressed to the slave owners they were not only losing valuable stock by hanging, but they might ignite a slave revolt or runaway, which would leave your crops and animals in disarray. Willie used a bag he brought with him to demonstrate his metaphor. He told them that in this bag he had a full proof method for controlling the Negros. He even guaranteed to everyone that if his methods were used properly, they would be able to control the Negro for at least 300 years. That meant their children's children would have great control over their most prized possession—the Negro. Willie said his methods had worked on his plantation and he knew they would work in the south, or anywhere there were slaves.

Willie noticed the differences of his slaves and made them bigger. He went on to explain he used fear, distrust and envy for control purposes. "On the top of my list is age—and this is only because age starts with an A and is the first letter in the alphabet." The crowd exploded in laughter. "The second on my list is color, or shade. There is intelligence, size, sex, sizes of plantation, status on plantation, attitude of owners, whether the slaves live in the valley, on the hill, east, west, north, south, have fine hair, course hair or is tall or short. These are all the differences of the Negro. Before I give you an outline of action, I will now tell you that, distrust is stronger than trust and envy is stronger than adulation, respect or admiration. After receiving this indoctrination the black slaves will carry on and will keep self-refueling and self-generating for hundreds of years—maybe thousands."

"It is paramount you pitch the old black male against the young black male, and the young black male against the old black male. You must use the dark skin slaves versus the light skin slaves, and the light skin slaves versus the dark skin slaves. You must use the female versus the male, and the male versus the female. You must also have white servants and overseers to distrust blacks. But it is necessary that your slaves thirst and depend on you. They must love, respect and trust only you."

Willie ended his speech by telling his cohorts to empower their wives and children with these control methods. He told the onlookers if they used these methods intensely for a year, the slave would remain perpetually distrustful. He closed his speech by saying, "Thank you, gentlemen."

Freddie Gavin

Larry knew the Willie Lynch speech very well. He studied it because it was a big part of the "Order" manifesto. Before a lad could be introduced to the body of the Order as a greenback (the first level of the Order), he had to read and understand the outline of the Willie Lynch letter. Larry had no problem learning the letter because he used to always love reporting back to his dad when he had an encounter with a black person and say, "Hey Poppa—Willie works!"

Destined to one day take his father's role in the hierarchy of the Order, Larry became intrigued with reading literature on days of the past and listening to the elders at the monthly meetings talking about how things use to be before the nigger rights movement took over. The elders use to call the Civil Rights Movement—the Nigger Rights Movement in honor of Reverend Dr. Martin Luther Koon. Larry even kept a copy of the letter pasted in his closet door so when he was searching for school clothes for the day he could read parts of the letter.

99

Chapter 9

GO FORTH SON

It was only one year removed from the historical President's

administration and the right-wing machine was pumping out venom

of hate so badly directed at the first African-American President.

Some of his most loyal supporters were wishing he would have

stayed a senator for fear of his life. The Righties were questioning

his citizenship because of his white mother and African father,

(interesting since the black race is called African-Americans) so

much so that he had to provide his birth certificate on national TV,

and despite that, the naysayers wouldn't quit. He was called a

Muslim, when it was clear he was a Christian. He was accused of

bowing down to world leaders. He was criticized for being smart.

Even candidates who were trying to secure the bid in the past

Republican Party primary race accused him of having bad grades in

college and getting into Harvard based on a quota system, when it was clear that, if challenged, half of the Republican candidates wouldn't be able to provide a decent SAT score.

All these accusations were directed at the new President when the country had just had in office a cowboy from Texas. In eight years George W. Bush ran up the deficit, started two wars, and cut taxes for his wealthy friends—while, mind you, causing an economic downspin so bad we were at the brink of a depression. Some analyst said we were in a recession. This self-appointed "decider," as he would call himself, was a reserve naval pilot who used his power of influence, his daddy, to keep him out of several combat conflicts. He admitted he didn't do well in school and his favorite subject was Jack Daniels and hanging out with his Bone and Skull fraternity brothers at Yale University. He took a balanced budget and destroyed it while stating he would change the world with his Christian values. Even his mother thought it wouldn't be a good idea for him to run for President.

With the rise of the Tea Party and stupid ass Norquest pledges, the Conservative party was becoming the party right of right. The Republican Party blocked ideas from the President even when they were the party who came up with the ideas years before President

Obama was born. Larry saw the writing on the wall. He knew being

in the Order, the rise of the Tea Party, and a black President would

play a significant part in crippling the Civil Rights Movement. He

knew this because of the recent historical election of America's first

black President. Hell, it was so bad you really couldn't tell a Tea

Party member from a Klan member.

He would always look to the heavens and say, "Lord, thank you

for Barrack Obama." This made Larry excited. He figured he would

take what he already knew about "control" to the Vanderbilt

University—learn from the educated elite of old and bring to the

fraternal Order a more advanced 21st century way of controlling the

niggers, because in his eyes, they were getting too smart and what he

would call, "Too fucking big-a-dee." Although his dad, Billy Ray,

wasn't pleased with Larry's decision to attend college, he knew

Larry was getting older and wanted more control over his life. He

also knew Larry had a secret that would destroy him. No, the secret

couldn't destroy him if a few blacks knew about it and tried to

expose him, but if a young, smart, pissed-off white boy who was next in line to be the next leader in the Order decided to expose his father's "dark secret," break all ties and expose the Order for what it was, it could be devastating; and Billy Ray didn't want that burden to bear. So with great skepticism, Billy Ray gave Larry his blessings to attend Vandy.

Chapter 10

THE SOUTHERN HARVARD

Like all freshmen, Larry went to orientation and stood in long

lines registering for his first semester of school. Larry was assigned

to the Crawford House. The Crawford House is a six story five-

year-old building located on what they called the Ingram Commons.

It houses about 150 first-year students in what is considered

traditional double rooms. Larry was excited about attending

Vanderbilt and was glad his roommate was not black.

Tommy Spencer was a marijuana smoking, long-haired, blue-

eyed, carefree, blonde kid from California. He didn't care about

Larry's hatred of blacks. He didn't care if Larry was in the Klan,

Order, or any other right-wing hate group. He was Larry's

roommate and for the most part had little in common with Larry.

The only thing he had in common with Larry was they were both

Caucasian, young, and freshmen at Vandy. The only thing that interested Tommy was getting back to California so he could go surfing and skate boarding with his friends. He knew he had to go to college so he chose Vanderbilt to see what his mother was making all the fuss about.

"Oh Tommy-boy, you should apply to one of the many great colleges in the south. And maybe you could spend some time with grandma, grandpa and some of your cousins you haven't seen since you were younger." His mother, Gloria, was from a city in Tennessee not far from Vanderbilt. Tommy thought he would honor his mother by attending a good school that wasn't far from her hometown and maybe take her up on her offer of visiting family. He remembered his childhood as visiting his grandparents and hanging out with his cousins and the other young kids in the area. He remembered the many times running up the road barefoot with his cousins and neighborhood kids, racing on the dirt roads, chasing behind trains on the nearby railroad, which was a stone's throw away, and boy, had they thrown many stones.

Tommy had fond memories of visiting his grandparents in the south. He also loved how friendly everyone seemed to be. Even when they would throw rocks at the main engine of the train, he could always see the conductor smiling and waving while blowing the loud engine whistle. Obviously the conductor knew something that a 10-year-old boy didn't—rocks didn't hurt metal, but the whistle sure scared the hell out of little 10 year old boys.

Larry and Tommy rarely talked at all. I think they may have said about three or four sentences to each other during the whole semester. But neither minded. As long as Larry didn't say anything to Tommy about his smoking habit and Tommy didn't say anything to Larry about some of the strange literature he saw on Larry's study desk, they were fine. However, one day out of curiosity Tommy asked Larry about what he thought were strange readings.

"Hey, roomie."

"Yeah, Kaliphonia." Larry said California like the word itself was gay.

"What's this stuff you reading? I mean, you got a right to read and hate anybody you want, but I was curious why would you subject yourself to that type of reading and ideology at a place where you know there is going to be some controversy—college."

106

"Well, surfer boy," another word Larry thought would insult his roomie, "it's a long story. You're not from the south, so you wouldn't understand how devious and conniving black people are. And if you are not careful—they might try to rob you."

Tommy found his statement pretty interesting, but creepy, because he knew most of the guys he hung out with in California were from all cultures. Although most of his surfing was done with his white buddies, he knew Rufus Smallwood was his best friend. Rufus taught him how to skateboard, and would do any and everything for his friend Tommy. But an important fact about Rufus was he was black. With Larry's statement, Tommy mumbled something under his breath and said, "Whatever dude." and that completed their extended conversation.

When Larry got his schedule, he looked it over to make sure he had a history class. He had the common freshman schedule: Math 1101, Science 2200 and Science lab 2201, English 1100 and History 1101. For an elective, he chose another history. He chose, History 2207, *"Battle Cry of Freedom: The Civil War Era."* I taught both history classes. He asked around and wanted to know who was the best history teacher that would challenge him and all the students he talked with and even the Registrar told him, "Dr. Truman." One student, an upper classman, told him, "Man—Dr. T is the shit! If you want to learn all the ends and outs about history, which I found boring—you're taking the right professor."

"You are lucky. Most of his classes go pretty quick."

With these many attributes, Larry knew his first year adviser had signed him up for the right class with the right professor. Boy, he knew he had hit the lottery.

Chapter 11

SURPRISE—I'M BLACK!

It was my first day of class and you would have thought I was

teaching for the first time. I always get excited about the new

students I meet from all over the world. Some of the kids were here

because it's a requirement—but some were here because they really

like history. It didn't matter to me; I just enjoyed teaching what I

like to call my little virgin historians. I guess the reason why I never

mentioned to anyone what I call my first-year history students, or

never tried to coin the phrase, was because people would probably

view me as some type of perverted pied piper waiting on the little

children to be mesmerized by my teaching so I could eventually

molest them after they were caught in my trap. I thought to

myself—how fucking sick!

My dad, rest his soul, used to always tell me you got to know

where you came from before you can know where you are going.

When I really thought about this simplistic saying, I came to the conclusion, "Damn, my dad made a lot of sense." No, Dad never won a Pulitzer or was nominated for a Nobel, but his many little sayings, although trivial, always made sense.

My first day of class was like any other day—or I thought it would be. Normally, when I walked into class you could hear crickets. Most of the little minds, although excited about their first day, were still a little nervous from anticipation on what to expect. I liked to walk in and at the same time welcome the kids and let them know who I was.

"Hello, students. First, I'd like to welcome you to one of the finest institutions in America."

Before I could mention my name, or grab their attention with my Eddie Murphy skit, a young white kid who was sitting in the first row blurted out, "NO FUCKING WAY!", and quickly overruled me.

"Excuse me?" Now the silence became even more silent. "As I was saying, my name is Dr. Truman. You can call me Dr. T, Dr. Truman or anything you think would be appropriate—just as long as you say Dr. first, because if you see the scars I received while earning my PhD, you would understand."

There was slight laughter and in the laughter you could hear someone say, "Can I call you Dr. Coon?"

I let the class go early on the first day because I knew there would be many days where their little brains would feel like they were going to explode. We went over the school rules, syllabus and the expectations I had for my class. After I released my last class for the day, I went home and reflected on some of the strange comments from one of the students. I told my wife Sara about the strange day and she asked me how I felt about it. I told her I really didn't know how to feel.

Sara Houston was short in statue, smart, beautiful and didn't like a lot of confrontation, or anything that would raise her blood pressure over 70. I knew I was going to marry her because of my mother's approval. My mother adored Sara, and Sara adored my mother. I can hear my mom before I got married say, "Boy, this one is a keeper." When my mother liked any female I brought home, I knew it was special. My mom never liked any female I introduced her to over the years—not one. But Sara—she thought she was the one for me—and she was. In all honesty, Sara reminded me of my

111

mother in many ways. I can hear one of my dad's sayings, "Boy, when you find a good woman that got your back—you better make her an honest woman." Sara had my back.

We met in undergrad, at Harvard. We spent a lot of time together in those early days. I use to practically live at her house. She was from West Medford and her parents reminded me of my parents. I recall Sara getting mad at me when I came over to her house.

"EJ—you can't come over to my house anymore!"

"Why gurl?"

"I don't know what you are telling my parents, but they are ready to adopt you if you gave them the ok. And poor dad—now that you are around all the time he thinks he can even the playing field with us girls."

Mr. Houston had three daughters. Even the dog was a girl. So the house was always filled with females. He loved me because I was the son he never had. He would take me places, show me around the city, and introduce me as his son. I thought that was funny but I didn't mind because he is a great man.

112

Sara and I married after she finished law school. When I took the job at Vanderbilt, she found a job as a corporate attorney for Wilson, Johnson, & Wilson. She has since made partner. Sara is my partner and best friend and when I have issues I always consult her free of charge for her assessment even though most of the time I don't listen. So when I told her about my strange first day at school, she did like she always did when I talk to her about an issue—she would ask me how I felt like I was a client in a psychiatrist clinic lying on the coach.

Larry was furious when he found out I was black. "A fucking NIGGER! How in the hell they let this coon teach here at Vandy? Sure they can teach gym, or coach—but a real class at Vandy? No fucking way! His black ass should be teaching at Be-Coon Cookman, or whatever they call that fucking nigger school!"

Bethune-Cookman is a historical black university in Florida. I think Larry must have seen the name somewhere. He was trying to be funny with the wrong pronunciation of Bethune Cookman. He paced back and forth in his room wondering what was going to be his next move. His roommate was lying on the bed smoking a joint and in a sly way laughing his ass off.

"Yo—dude, calm down! Here, take a drag!" Larry didn't get high and Tommy knew that. He was just trying to be comical.

Tommy knew how Larry felt about black people and he was ecstatic when he found out Dr. Truman was black. To Tommy, that was what he thought his roomie needed. He thought, "That's what that racist bastard needs. He claims he reads so fucking much."

He looked at Larry, who had just sat down on his bed looking like he just gave birth and sarcastically said, "Man—when I have a problem with the blacks and it makes me upset like it got you, I read one of my favorite books by Harriet Beecher Stowe—Uncle Tom's Cabin." Larry didn't know how to take his roommate.

Tommy knew this book was filled with a bunch of stereotypes of black people.

"Man have you ever read it?"

"No."

"Check it out of the library and give it a try—I think it would help you deal with black people better." What Tommy didn't tell his

114

racist roomie was that the same book was also credited with helping fuel the abolitionist cause in the 1850s.

"Sure, man—I'll check it out!"

Tommy got up from smoking the blunt, put on some jeans and an old skull face T-shirt, some flip-flops, looked at his dumbass roomy, shook his head as he was going out the room and said, "Later." As Tommy was leaving the room, he couldn't help but think, "How in the hell did I get put in the same room with fucking David Dukes Jr.? I need to find a Black Panther group and invite them over to my room for pizza."

For weeks little crazy disrespectful outbursts would occur in the classroom and my suspicions rose that it was number 45. It wasn't anything that I couldn't handle. Although I could look around the room and see into some student's eyes who felt a little uncomfortable with 45's antics, the outbursts were harmless. Since there were over 150 pupils in my room, I had a system where I drew up a type of schematic of seating arrangements and the kids who were sitting in those chairs were assigned to those seats by numbers.

Until I got to learn their names, I would just call on them by their number. I would eventually, over time, learn their names, but that took at least two weeks. Well, that was for the ones who were brave enough to come back. I would always think, "How in the hell could anyone would be so disrespectful to me? Shit, these kids love me. I was voted faculty professor of the year 10 years straight. Well, he must not have been hugged as a child."

It was December 5, we were getting close to the end of the semester, and kids were getting antsy because they finally were getting a chance to take a break from school and spend some time home with their friends and family. One morning before class had started, Mr. Bailey approached me while I was sitting in my office. I found it a little odd Mr. Bailey would come by my office, walk past my secretary and close my door. Although he and I talked on a regular basis before and after class and would grab a bite to eat every now and then, this was the first time he had ever walked in my office with a look of disgust on his face.

"Mr. Bailey, how are you doing?"

"EJ, other than getting old, I'm feeling good." We both gave a little laugh about that.

"How can I help you today?"

"Well son, I'm really here on your behalf."

"What's wrong?"

"This morning, when I was cleaning your office I saw where someone had written on your board—"NIGGERS ARE DESTROYING THIS COUNTRY AND MY FRIEND WILLE LYNCH IS NOT PLEASED!""

Mr. Bailey arrives at the university probably before the campus police change third shift.

"I wanted to not only tell you about this but I wanted you to see it."

I got up from what I was doing--I think I was looking at my emails--and headed down to my classroom with Mr. Bailey. Sure enough, there it was in very bold letters. They even had the audacity to use different colors for special effects. Mr. Bailey also handed me a noose that was placed on the back of my chair with a picture of my face near it. He looked at me and said, "These damn people! No matter what you do in this God forsaken country, there will always be bigots and fools trying to destroy us."

I looked at Mr. Bailey and could see he was visibly upset. I wondered if he was thinking about all the racism he had to endure when he was a young man and as an adult.

"Son, do you want me to call campus?" Campus was the name everyone called the campus police—it made things a little softer than saying police.

"No, sir. I know just what to do."

"I'll see you later, son." Mr. Bailey said.

"O.K., Mr. Bailey."

Chapter 12

IT'S TIME

I was so pissed off at number 45—Larry Dixon. I was just

pissed off at the whole fucking system of injustice that is always in

some form or fashion delivered through white privilege. It seems as

if when white people are challenged by their own system of justice

they turn into their symbol of hope, the bald eagle, in high skies

searching and looking for prey to devour. Diving down from

sometimes a half mile with eyes fixated on its prey like a high

powered scope on a sniper rifle, traveling at speeds in excess of over

100 miles an hour, quickly sweeping its prey off its feet, and taking

it back to its nest to demolish any time it pleases.

Their system of justice was built on a hierarchy of control and

justice and blacks were somewhere at the bottom; not lower than dog

shit, but not higher than white children. From slavery, to the many

lynchings of millions of African-Americans—from the Civil Rights

119

Movement to Jim Crow—I was tired! From Brown v. Board of

Education, to Plessey v. Ferguson, from the three little black girls

killed in an Alabama church, to the three young civil rights activists

found murdered in Mississippi—I was tired! I was tired of the

newly black President, my classmate, having to prove himself at

every turn. I was tired of a country that was built on the backs of

slave labor and the only credit that is revered in American history

books are based on a few blacks who tried to change an

unchangeable cause. Even after their most prized possession, the

Constitution of the United States, which most Americans look upon

as if it was the Art of the Covenant, blacks find themselves

struggling to be accepted in the 21st century.

I was tired of being in a country that could adopt Christianity and

for over 400 years use it to justify its mistreatment of first the natives

and then blacks, or any immigrant who was of color. I used to

always think as a young boy of the pain Jesus must be suffering; but

not of the suffering he endured on the cross 2000 years ago for

mankind, but of the hardship and mistreatment he sees of his people

of color in America. My conclusion is most white people who were born in America have a pride rooted in faith, not necessarily in God, and a sense of privilege unwavering and unmatched in their existence. When it came to exercising their rights against other races, they think black people shouldn't have the same rights as they do. They take pride in their heritage and always believed they are God's chosen people—not the Jews of past. I have heard many white folk express their hatred against racism. I even have white friends who claim they have never had a racist bone in their body. Many of my white colleagues express things are better for the African-American race. "Hey, EJ!" They would say. "Racism is a thing of the past. *We* even elected an African-American President" As if they (white folk) are the final arbiters of whether a black person should be President. Hell, if you got to say things are better and use the word *we* as if it's the standard, then things hadn't got better. Maybe better in the sense of visual racism, but not in the worst way of racism—the unseen.

When I heard my white colleagues say this, I would say to myself, "I'll take mine visual." I knew they meant well, but when you are born into a world of privilege, you really can't see the big

121

picture. Racism is still prevalent today as it was many years ago.

There are two types of racism, the first being explicit racism—the type that everyone sees and talks about. A good example of that would be number 45, my confused student. This is the type of racism that is easily identified, which means there's hope for the culprit. The other type of racism is implicit. Implicit racism is very scary. It's rooted deep within the mind of the culprit. Actually, it's so deep rooted that the culprit doesn't even know that they are being racist. It's one of those things where you have colleagues making dumbass comments about racism being purged because of one half black/white President. The scary part about implicit racism is it's even a chameleon to the people that are being attacked.

There is nothing new about master servant ideology. Over millions of years, even during biblical times, one race of people has always served another race of people. The poor have always been against the rich and the rich have always looked down on the poor. I understood that. But this primitive way of thinking has caused a cancer so devastating and deeply rooted, not only has it spread throughout the world and spanned through many centuries, it has festered in our most prized commodity—our soul. Once a cancer

festers in your mind and soul it spreads faster than stage four cancer.

The only thing we can do is pray the morphine used to ease the pain

in hospice helps with the certain death. So when Mr. Bailey wanted

to go get "Campus" because of the recent incidents I had

encountered, I told him I knew what to do. I knew it was time to put

the gift I got from God to use.

Chapter 13

1800s

Class was a little different than usual, not because I was

teaching anything new but because there were only a few days left in

school. It was finals week, and the kids were getting ready to go

home for the holiday. I had the usual kids. About half were good

students and a little more than half were average. Then there were

the ones who weren't coming back next year, or the ones who I

would see sometime before they graduated because they had to take

my class over again. I paid special attention to Larry's grades. The

interesting thing about his grades was that he maintained the highest

grade point average in my class and when I inquired about his grades

to some of the other professors, they all expressed to me he was a

pleasant student and had great grades. My first thought was, "I

know Larry was only pleasant to the other professors because they

were white." Then I thought, "For this young man to be such a jerk, I

must say he is really bright."

When class let out, I conveyed to the kids what was going to be on the final exam and told them to study hard. I also asked Larry would he come by my office later that day. He reluctantly said, "What time?"

"What time is good for you Mr. Dixon?"

"What about twelve tonight?" He said twelve as if that was the time he had made the uninvited visit to my classroom and left me the unwanted pleasantries on my blackboard and seat.

"No, Mr. Dixon, I'll see you at 4 sharp."

"Sure, man, whatever." Larry knew he would be there because when it came to his grades, he was an over achiever. He also knew I was, as he would say, the nigger that was giving him his history grade.

I was just finishing up some of the administration work I was assigned when I heard a knock on my door. "Come on in."

"Hey, Dr. Truman—you wanted to see me?" He actually said this like he liked me.

"Sit down Larry." Without telling him why I wanted to see him, I started lecturing. "Son, I know it was you who wrote the terrible message on the blackboard. I also know it was you who left the noose in my seat. And for the last few weeks, I've been hearing the small, under your breath, racial slurs you make while I'm writing on the blackboard. Larry, I understand and I'm aware we as Americans have a Constitution, which allows us freedom of expression, however, that freedom is not absolute—especially in my classroom while I'm trying to teach."

Larry was looking down on the floor as if he had spotted a twenty-dollar bill and was waiting on the right opportunity to pick it up. He looked as if he were thinking, "Nigger the Constitution wasn't really written for you; it was revised because of Yankees and Lincoln."

"Son, you are a bright young man, and I found out you have aspirations of one day teaching history." I was sure he was interested in history; I wasn't sure about him wanting to teach it.

"So, Mr. Dixon, what should I do with you?" Larry looked at me and knew that I knew he was the culprit of the incident.

"Mr…. I, I," he said stuttering, "I mean Dr. Truman…it was just a joke."

126

Freddie Gavin

Looking at Larry, I could see he was visibly shaken.

"Son—I'm not going to press charges or even tell Campus." Larry looked surprised. "I'll tell you what, you tell me why you did it and we will move forward from here."

"Well, truthfully, Dr. Truman, I'm a product of my environment." I knew what Larry was trying to say, but now since he wasn't saying it under his breath in class or around his redneck friends in McCormick, South Carolina, it was hard for him to tell me what "product" meant.

So I pushed him. "Son, I don't understand what you mean. I'm going to give you one more chance to be truthful. If you are not truthful, I will call Campus and let them figure this whole blackboard and noose thing out."

"Well, Dr. Truman—I—I…Well, I hate niggers—I mean African-Americans." He looked at me as if he was waiting on me to strike him or pick up the phone and call Campus. When he saw I didn't seem upset, he let out a sigh of relief.

"So why do you have this hatred for African-Americans?"

127

He tried to give me this bullshit story about his upbringing and where he lived. That's how he was raised and—so on and so forth—the same old tired answer you would get from any white person who has just been called out about their hatred of African-Americans.

"So, Larry, what are you going to do about it?" This is normally my method of counseling young people who come to me for advice, or for discipline. I try to make them think about what they are really saying and ask them about their problem with a question.

"Well, what I really want to happen can't."

"And what's that?"

"I would like to have been around during slavery and possibly meet my idol Willie Lynch."

I looked him straight in the eye and asked him, "Do you really wish you could have been around during slavery to meet Willie Lynch?"

He looked at me like I didn't hear him the first time and said, "Yes, sir. I would have loved to have met Willie Lynch. I wish I was back during the time when Mr. Lynch was running things."

"Oh, you think things would be better for you if you were around during slavery and wouldn't have to deal with all these uppity Negros here in the 21st century right?"

"Yes, sir. I know things would be different—but I know that's not possible."

"O.K., Larry, your wish has been granted." Before Larry could respond to me granting his request, I honored his request and teleported him to 1850.

"Boy, get yo' black azz up!" When Larry blinked his eyes, they opened to the screaming of a slave-owner handler. He couldn't understand why this white man, his brother in race, was yelling at him and calling him degrading names. He was wondering where this guy came from. He thought, "Did I fall asleep on Dr. Truman while we were talking?" But Larry wasn't in my office. Larry had wanted to meet Willie Lynch since his reading and understanding of the famous Lynch letter. What he couldn't believe was he was going to meet his hero, but not as a white, good ole southern redneck from McCormick, South Carolina; but as a black slave from Benin, West Africa.

129

Larry was still in shock and confused about not being able to identify his whereabouts and the mistreatment he was receiving from whom he thought was a professor. He thought, "Who is this guy talking to?"

Once he realized the slave handler was talking to him, he responded, "Who are you?" Before Larry could get the word 'you' out of his mouth, the slave handler slapped him with such force Larry's lip and nose started bleeding. Confused and frustrated, Larry stayed silent until he could get his bearings. He thought, "Let's see—I was just in Dr. Truman's office."

"Boy, I'm only going to tell your black azz one more time, get the fuck up!" Larry got up from what was once a chair and now was a bale of hay, and was stunned at what he had just realized—he wasn't in my office and the guy that had just slapped him wasn't a professor.

"That's right, boy—that's right! Now you being a good nigger!" The slap in the face couldn't prepare Larry for what he had just realized. Not only was he far removed from my office, when he looked at his clothes they were old clothes from the slavery era. However, when he looked at his hands and feet, he realized he was still white but caught up in some sick dream where he was a black slave in the 1850s.

"You are done here. Now git your azz back to the field! Fucking niggers always trying to rest when they should be working!"

Although still a little confused, Larry started heading back in the direction of where he thought the field would be. A little boy name Bucky saw Larry was acting kind of spooked so he called out to him, "Hey, James." Larry kind of looked around. "Yea, yuh, James. Marster Andy wuz kina hard on you but you got to lissen. Come on wit me—I take you back." Larry followed the young black boy back to the field where he was led to an older very skinny, dark-skinned man name Clarence.

"James, what wrong wit you! You act spooked."

Pretending like he had saw a ghost, Larry said, "Yeah, I fell and hit my head and Master Andy wasn't too kind with that."

"I thawt you waz helpin' Marster Andy?"

"I was but he sent me back to the field when I fell."

"Oh! Come on, den, let's git back to work—you know Marster Lynch want his harvest picked befo' end of harvest!"

"O.K." Not only was Larry devastated he was now a slave in 1850, it was hard for him to understand the language of his new cohorts.

Larry had never in his life experienced the kind of backbreaking work like he was experiencing in his new profession—slavery. Not just any slave, but a field slave. The joy of slavery brought us two types of slavery. You were either considered a lower class slave or the more prestigious higher-class slave; Larry was a lower class slave. A lower class slave was considered a field slave. Being a field slave provided you with the very grueling work of picking cotton, tobacco, or any crop that kept the southern economy moving. Most slaves would be up from sunup until sundown in the hot fields working. Many times the field slaves worked in the fields 10 to 18 hours a day, constantly monitored by overseers. Larry was working on Mr. Lynch's plantation. Mr. Lynch had over 500 acres of cotton, which provided his 300 slaves an average production of about 100 pounds of clean cotton a day per slave. This was long, tedious, arduous, backbreaking work and Larry didn't think he would make it through the day.

The overseer or slave handler would make sure the work Mr. Lynch's slaves were doing didn't slow down or cease until the workday was over. Mr. Lynch was a tyrant to his slaves. However, he knew exactly how to treat them to get the most work out of them. Most slave owners not only worked their slaves until the day was over, but in some cases some were worked to death. If things were not running smoothly or someone was not working enough, the slave would be whipped by the handler. Even pregnant enslaved women could not escape duties in the field. They would have to work up until the delivery of the baby and right after delivery of the baby.

The clothing the field slaves were given was terrible. Field s aves were given the bare minimum to cover their bodies, and were only given one winter set of clothes and one summer set of clothes. Their living conditions were not much better. They lived in one-room cabins with their whole family. The cabins had mud floors with roofs that usually leaked and in the winter filled with smoke because of the fireplace. They slept on straw mattresses. They were fed only once a day with a diet consisting of cornmeal and fatty meat, or sometimes whatever their master chose to give them.

Many times, there was animosity between the field slaves and the house slaves. Larry knew this reason all too well. He knew from reading the Lynch letter that the house slaves on occasion acted as spies for the slave owners. He thought to himself over and over again how in the hell did he find himself in this predicament. Then it clicked— "Dr. Truman—that's it! All I need to do is find Dr. Truman and this nightmare would be over. That's what I got to do—find Dr. Truman."

What Larry didn't realize was I had given him a gift. The gift to meet his hero, Willie Lynch; the gift to see, feel, and be black— and the gift to know what true racism feels like. And once he experienced this 1850 phenomena, I wanted him to know that if he didn't take off his blinders of racial injustice and see that his world was based on bigotry and racist demagoguery, would only be a classroom away from sending him on another realism expedition to visit another one of his southern heroes. However, this adventure wasn't over.

Chapter 14

MY HERO

Because of many unforeseen conditions that were starting to

plague Willie's plantation, he decided to reassess his most prized

commodity, the Negro. Willie was losing slaves faster than he could

produce a profitable earning on his plantation and he realized that

was bad for business. Willie thought hard about the importance of

the slaves and realized he was making a grave mistake in the way he

was managing them. Willie thought, "I'm losing slaves as fast as I

can buy them—some are even starting to rebel and runaway—I got

to change my plan!" He set down in his study with pen and paper

and devised a scheme he believed if done properly would change

the thinking of the slave, and the slave-owners would have control

over their slaves for centuries to come.

Willie studied the slave as if he was a student that was one semester away from getting his PhD. He knew his thesis had to be spot-on if he was going to try to put his thoughts in practice. He wrote about everything from the physical to the psychological aspect of the slave. He understood slavery was a business—big business! He also knew slaves were humans, although they were sometimes treated less than humans. Willie's thoughts captured all the do's and don'ts on how to properly "make a slave." His writings incorporated the use of fear, distrust, and envy as a controlling mechanism to his most prized chattel. Willie met with all of his handlers and gave them strict instructions on what he expected from them. He told them if they did their jobs and followed his new instructions it would not only benefit him, but also them. He promised the handlers something they could understand—more money.

In 1821, the summer before Willie's 35th birthday, he put his plan to the test using his plantation. The test was a success. Willie was ecstatic knowing he now had the key to making his plantation a

137

more profitable entity. In fact, he was so successful, he was asked

by political pundits to speak to other slave owners who were having

problems with their slaves. Later that year, Willie spoke to a crowd

of about a few hundred slave-owners on the banks of the James

River in Virginia about the making of a slave.

"James, yuh need to go to the big house. Mr. Lynch need yuh and

a few others."

It was about 7 that night and James was just getting out of the

field from a long hard day when he was summoned to the big house.

James thought, "Shit! What the FUCK?" Then he realized he wasn't

in Kansas anymore. He responded, "Yessuh!" He knew if he

wouldn't have responded properly it could have caused him a

whipping or maybe a shortage on food rations.

He got to the big house and saw a man sitting on the porch in a

white rocking chair, smoking a pipe. The temperature still was about

90 degrees that late in the evening and this white man on the porch

was wearing a white suit and white hat. James thought, "Damn, I

thought Colonel Sanders was dead." James knew he had to find humor where ever he could because he knew most of his time on

the plantation was far from any comedy house he had ever seen or

heard about. He had never seen Mr. Lynch because the history

books didn't have any pictures of him and since his magical time

warp to the plantation, thanks to me, this would be his first time

meeting his hero.

"Hi, sir. I was told you needed me?" James was standing in front

of Willie, afraid to look on the elevated porch at him.

"I certainly do. How have you been treated since you've been

here?"

James thought, "He said that to me as if he and Dr. Truman were

in on this together." Before James answered, he looked around as

to see if I was going to come around the porch and say, "Okay, son,

you can wake up now."

"Well", he paused, "Pretty good."

Willie was trying to feel James out. He knew if James would have

answered in a semi-smart way he wouldn't be a good candidate for

his next mission. Willie always needed spies and he was trying to test and question James to see if he would be a good candidate to continue with his biddings. "Are they feeding you good?"

Although James wanted to say hell no, he just said, "Yes, sir."

"Good!"

"Look—James right?"

"Yes, sir."

"I have been watching you for a while and because you are such a good worker, I would like to give you something else to do."

James didn't know what to say, so he just nodded his head in agreement.

"Because of your hard work, I'm gonna let you be over some of your people. Would you like that?"

"Yes, sir."

"I heard Andy gave you a hard time a spell back so I will talk to him about that." He knew about the Andy incident but he really didn't care. Willie was a very smart and cunning man and he knew the way to the slave was through their psyche. He only mentioned the incident because he wanted James to feel like he had his back.

140

"James, I will make sure you get some extra clothes and food rations with your new duties."

James was to be an Underling. An Underling was a trusted slave that was over other slaves. The only person they answered to was the Overseers. When Willie was just finishing up his talk with James, Andy arrived. "Mr. Lynch you wanted to see me?"

"Andy, two things—James, here will be going over to Randall. He will be an Underling; I have already talked with Randy about that." That's what everyone called Randall—Randy. "And another th ng, the next time I hear about you hurting another one of my slaves you will be looking for another job on another plantation and I promise you won't find a plantation within a thousand miles that would take you—understand?"

"Yes, sir."

This was some type of mental game to Willie. He wouldn't get rid of Andy and Andy kind of knew this. Although extremely mean toward the slaves, Andy was Willie's best overseer. He had to tone down his mistreatment of slaves since Willie's new and improved how to instructions, but every now and then he would show the slaves no mercy. The slaves even had a name for Andy—Apepi, which meant serpent demon.

Andy left like a wounded animal. "Now, James, I'm counting on you."

"Yes, sir."

"Oh—one more thing—if you hear any of the slaves talking about leaving or anything you know is not good for them let me know. You see, James, I want to treat the nigger fair and the only way I can do that is when you hear something, you come straight to me and tell me all about it. That way I can try to talk to them and make things right like I did with you and Andy. O.K.?"

"Yes, sir."

James thought, "Is this the man that I wanted to be? He is just as bad as my dad—a wolf in sheep's clothing. Mother-Fucker!"

Mr. Lynch looked at James and said, "Ok—you need to git back now."

"Yes, sir."

142

James became friendly with many of the field and house slaves. He couldn't believe the only thing that made them different from him and when he was back in his world was opportunity. James would constantly think about being home, but he would quickly dispel that thought because he knew if he thought of home too often he wouldn't survive in his new environment. He would often think about how he mistreated a lot of the African-Americans in his hometown. He thought of how bad he and the slaves were being treated here in the 1800s. He thought about the deceit that was being displayed by Willie Lynch and came to the conclusion that he was a fraud. He did as Willie asked and when he saw something, he went to him and let him know what was going on in the slave community. He also used his method of deceit by not telling the whole truth, but telling in a way that seemed minor. James had to be careful about which slaves he could tell because Willie had the slaves so divided most of them only trusted him. The slaves he could trust he told; the slaves he couldn't tell, he did not.

James recalled a few weeks back what they did to a Negro that he couldn't trust. He told Mr. Lynch the Negro, Willie Lee, was planning on running. They brought Willie Lee back from the woods, chained like a wild boar. Mr. Lynch's overseers and trusted Negros were the best hunters and catchers in the world. Willie Lee was fast and thought he would leave the plantation at night. However, what Willie Lee didn't know was they knew he was trying to run and were waiting on his departure. They allowed Willie Lee a three-hour head start and caught him before sunrise the next day. The next day, Willie Lynch had a beating and boiling party for Willie Lee. Any time Willie Lynch would severely punish a slave, he would make sure he did it where everyone could see—all the slaves (children included) his family, everyone.

Willie had many methods of punishment, but I guess he was feeling a little good this day. James watched in horror as they stripped Willie Lee of his clothes, tied him to a tree like he was Christ, and two of his overseers, which included Andy, whipped him from front to back. They would beat him unconscious and when he

144

woke they would start whipping him again. This would go on for at

least an hour. I guess that was an appetizer because what they did

next stayed with James.

They dragged Willie over to a very large pot that was boiling and

ask Willie Lee did he want to apologize to Mr. Lynch. James thought,

"Apologize. How in the hell is he going to do this when they literally

just beat almost every inch of his life from his body for trying to run

away from hell!"

Willie Lee was bleeding so badly that the only thing he could do

was nod his head up or down. Andy asked Willie Lee again, "BOY—

do you hear me." Andy loved humiliating the slaves—they knew

this, he knew this and the owner of the plantation knew this.

James thought Willie Lee was going to look up and answer Andy,

but when he didn't answer the second time, Andy and Bo Bo picked

him off the ground and started putting him in the pot as if he was

the last and main ingredient of a tasty stew. The screams were

deafening, and the smell was unbelievable. Willie Lee, a runaway

slave who had a woman and four kids, was whipped and boiled to

145

death on that hot summer day in front of them and the entire

plantation, and there was nothing anyone could do to stop it. James

again thought that the smell was horrible and the screams were

something that would stay with him for a lifetime.

After the "Festival of Boiling," Willie stood before the plantation

and gave this bullshit speech about trust and honesty and how he

thought he treated the slaves well. He went on about how he saw

the slaves like family. James thought, "What family is he talking

about?" He even had a tear coming out of his eyes when Willie Lee

was being boiled alive. James thought, "What a cynical son-of-a-

bitch!" After this horrible display of Lynch love, James was

desperate to return back to his humble beginnings, back to

McCormick, South Carolina and college.

Mr. Lynch also summoned James and praised him for being the

kind of slave that not only made him proud, but also was the type of

slave that was going to make his race see him as a hero.

James couldn't believe his hero was not the man he admired. He

wasn't even a wolf in sheep clothing like his father. James realized

146

the man who he admired, the man who he thought he wanted to be, the man who he thought the Order tried to use as a modern day symbol for controlling African-Americans wasn't a man at all. James thought his idol was the devil's father himself on earth.

James got back from the incident and had a feeling of horror he would never forget and realized—he was in hell. He understood the people he hated so much were his people. He understood slaves were taken from their land and forced to do things that weren't right. James thought, "Whether they were sold into slavery from wars in their country, or captured by slave traders and bought back to America, they have had a terrible journey." He thought about killing Willie Lynch and suffering the consequences, but he realized he was a coward and his toughness and strength came from being white and having American white privilege. He thought about everything and he really wanted to change the way he looked at African-Americans. He wanted to thank Dr. Truman for giving him something he knew, if all of his white friends and family had experienced would change their lives. He set next to his straw bec

147

and thought about home and went to sleep with a smile on his face. James was at peace.

The next day before James was to head to the field as the new handler of a group of about 40 slaves, he was summoned to Mr. Lynch's study. It was rare that Mr. Lynch would allow any field slave to come that far into the big house. However, Mr. Lynch took a liking to James. As James was going to the big house he thought he had better get used to being here and although he knew he was Bubba, a white boy from another dimension, he was now O.K. with being James the Negro handler.

"Hello Massa Lynch."

"Come on in, James." Like always, Mr. Lynch would always start out with pleasantries and it didn't matter whether you were black or white.

"How have you been?"

"I feel good, suh."

"Are they treating you good?"

"Yes, suh."

"Do you like what you are doing?"

"Yes, suh."

"I heard something and I was wondering did you hear the same thing. I heard a few of my new slaves were planning a revolt." Mr. Lynch thought out loud, "Even after I whip and boil a nigger for the world to see there's always a few—Goddammit!" James just held his head down in silence.

"Have you heard anything?"

"I sho did."

"Excuse me?"

"I mean –I sure did." And before Mr. Lynch could say you black bastard, James said," And I am the one who is leading the charge—you sick fucker!"

Mr. Lynch couldn't believe what he was hearing from his new prided Negro. He knew his method of making a slave was a success, but he couldn't understand why this slave was talking to him this way.

James replied, "You used to be my hero, I know everything about you and I know what you told the slave owners on the bank in Virginia. I know it has been working for a few hundred years."

Lynch look at James, befuddled. He was baffled at what James was saying. He reached into his drawer and pulled out his revolver and said, "You stupid nigger!" He quickly walked around the other side of his desk to where James were standing and hit James in the head with the butt of his revolver, knocking him out.

Chapter 15

REDEMPTION

"Larry—Larry—LARRY!" I called him three times and

when he looked up and saw it was me you would have thought he

had seen a ghost. Without saying a word, Larry jumped out of my

couch and gave me a bear hug and wouldn't let go.

"Larry—are you O.K.?"

Larry was still hugging me with enough force to cut off my

circulation.

"O.K., Larry, it's OK."

Still in shock, but hugging me with a little less tension, Larry

replied, "Is it really you, Dr. Truman?"

"Yes, Larry, it's me."

"Did I really meet Willie Lynch? Was it really real?"

"Slow down, son. Yes, you really did meet Willie Lynch. I gave

you a great gift. The gift to see what African-Americans had to endure many years ago. I also gave you the gift to see what it felt like to be a slave."

First Larry looked at me as to say 'a gift—more like a nightmare,' but then it clicked.

"Dr. Truman, what was I thinking?"

Although Larry was only transformed to slavery for a few hours, to him it seemed like he was gone for a few years. Larry reflected on his recent experience as a slave and replied, "Dr. Truman, how can I change?"

"Larry, it's not an easy thing for anyone to make a change, especially when your whole life experience and most of your culture has been cultivated on an ideology of hate. First, I think you need to go and meditate on what you think the word 'change' means to you."

Larry looked at me like I had suggested he go back and take a second look at slavery and the Willie Lynch experience. I told Larry to take a hard reflection on his life and to read a book by Tim Wise, *White Like Me, and Dear White America: Letter to a New Minority*. I told him these books would give him a white perspective of how race plays an issue within the white community as it relates to

152

African-Americans. I advised him this would be a start for him. I told him if he read these books and did a 15-page paper from his readings on them, I would give him full credit for my class. I told him I would set up some sensitivity training from Mr. Wise, since I knew him personally. I also advised him if and when he returned to school after the holiday break he didn't need to take the remainder of my class. I ended our conversation by telling him I would always be there for him if he needed to talk. Larry left my office and made the quarter of a mile walk back to his room.

"What's up, roomie? It looked like you've seen a ghost. Did you get a chance to go by the library and check out the book I was telling you about?"

"No, maybe later before I go home for break."

Tommy was all packed and ready to get back to the beaches of liberal bliss. Even in the winter, Tommy knew that the surf would be up and the water on the beach would be warm enough to enjoy. It was unusual for Tommy to chatter so much, but he was excited about going home. "Well, I hope you have a great break and I'll see you when I get back."

Larry was all alone in his room, reflecting on what Dr. Truman had told him. He knew he had many challenges ahead of him but he knew he had to do something. He packed his belongings he was taking home for the break, made a quick stop to the library to check out Tim Wise's books and started his six hour journey home.

The six hour drive would take Larry about ten hours. He spent most of the time thinking about his experience. He thought about how the once most respected man he looked up to was just a lie. He thought about his half-sister Penny and how horrible it must have been for Miss Valarie to have conceived her from being raped by his dad. He thought about his mother who allowed these horrible things to go on with silence. He thought about his girlfriend whom he knew didn't like how he was acting towards African-Americans. When he finished thinking about all of his many problems, he would start all over and think of them again. He knew he had to do something and he was ready to face his fears.

Chapter 16

THE HOMECOMING

Larry got home late in the evening and was greeted by his

mom. His dad was hunting with friends and although he knew his

son was coming home he wanted to show Larry his dislike for going

to college by not being there when he arrived. Larry greeted his

mom and they went in the study to talk about most of the things he

had learned at the southern Harvard.

"Larry, you hungry, baby?"

"Yes, mother." Larry always called his mom mother as if he was

living in the EU.

"I cooked a good meal for you, and dad should be home in a few

hours." Larry's mom was just like any other southern-belle. A great

housekeeper who loved God, family, and followed every word of her

husband even when she knew those words were flawed.

Larry dreaded the fact he had to see his father but he was ready to

face him and confront him about the brainwashing techniques he used from birth to corrupt his young mind into believing in such a horrible way to treat people—especially African-Americans.

The phone rang and Larry answered.

"What's up, college boy?" His friend Thomas said.

"Hey, Thomas, what's up wit you?"

"Man, let's go hang out at the spot and harass some niggers—oh, I'm starting police academy in a few weeks."

He knew more about Larry than anyone except his parents. Although Thomas' disdain for blacks wasn't good, he knew his hatred wasn't promulgated by hate as much as it was by the fear he had of his other cohorts. Larry was the ringleader and Thomas knew it. Thomas only stated what he thought Larry wanted to hear. When Larry didn't respond to Thomas's request, and only replied he would talk with him later, Thomas knew something was terribly strange about his friend.

Larry laid across his bed reflecting again on his slavery trip and all the people he had to confront and fell asleep.

"Larry—Larry!" Larry's mother called out his name and went to his room with a tray of food in her hands. She had made his

156

favorite—southern fried chicken, potato salad, green beans, and

sweet tea. She called once more before she entered the room and

saw him asleep across the bed. She put the food tray down on a

table next to his bed, looked at her son, covered him with the blanket

that was folded at the end of his bed, and left the room. Larry slept

what seemed like an eternity.

Chapter 17

PREGAME

The south is synonymous with football, trucks, the

Confederate flag, and church. Most white southerners pride

themselves on being rednecks. They perceive the word redneck as a

word of endearment. Rednecks in the south identify each other by

their trucks, the Confederate flag, hunting, and their love for

football. The South Eastern Conference, or the SEC as it is called, is

everything to a southern white male over the age of two. It's bred in

them just as much as racial justification is used in their disdain to the

African-American culture. Whether at work, or a party, or hunting,

the talk in any conversation of a southern good ole boy will always

capture, "What is Georgia football doing?" "How will Mark Richt

do this year?" "What boys he got coming in?" "Who does South

Carolina have coming in as freshman?" It goes on and on like this

through every conversation. Hunting, trucks and football; it is the way of life in the south. The thing that always seemed funny to me was although the southern good ole boys loved SEC football, most of the guys that were stars on these respective football squads were mostly African-Americans. I wouldn't be far off if I were to say about 90 percent of the players were black and about 90 percent of the coaches and coaching staff were white. It reminded me of the old slave to master relationship—or a master slave role.

The masters, or the overseers, would go to the auction block and buy what they thought would be a good hard working nigger, similar to the head coaches and assistant coaches of a team going to a high school game and watching the game, or going to a practice and taking notes on a player. When the time was right, these coaches would go to the star athlete's home and try to convince the player that their school was the one for them—sometimes gifts and money would follow shortly after the coach's visit.

"Bang—Bang!"

"Got- Dammit!" Billy Ray thought out loud to himself, "I been out here all day—had a chance to shoot the big one and missed by a mile—FUCK!" Billy Ray called Smitty on his two-way hunting radio. "Ray to Smitty."

"What's up, Ray—over?"

"10-4—I'm packing it in." Billy and John Smith, one of Billy's working buddies and friends, had been hunting all day. They normally got to their hunting lodge about 5 in the morning. The hunting lodge was 300 acres, secluded, gated, and somewhat of a resort located on Billy Ray's property that had been in his family since the Civil War. Although they hunted, they normally went there to get away from things and watch football, play cards, or any other thing they wanted to do. They even had Order meetings there, and on occasion they hunted.

Ray and Smitty got back to the lodge about 20 minutes after the radio call. Billy sat around with some of the fellows with Smitty and chit chatted for a few before he took the forty-five minute drive home. After about thirty minutes of chatting, Billy said his salutations and was on his way home. Billy was in no rush to get home because he knew his son was home for the Christmas break and he still was upset with his son for going a different direction from what he wanted him to do.

Billy turned his car radio to talk radio just to hear what his favorite shock jock was talking about. And not to disappoint, Rush Limbaugh was blasting Obama about everything. Every word that Rush exposed seemed like poetry to Billy Ray. Rush Limbaugh—an 80 million dollars a year, drug using, draft dodging, fat boy, whose only mission in life is to have middle-aged and old white working-class poor and rich men vote against their economic interests—is a hero to most guys like Billy Ray. Billy Ray thought, "Hell, Rush should be the President—not that destroying socialist from Kenya "

Two minutes from home Billy Ray figured he had better get into the mood to address his disrespectful son. Although Billy Ray was mad at his son, he knew he loved his son. He knew he was smart and able to make rational decisions on his own. He knew one day when Larry finished college he would take over the family business and continue the struggle against the government, whom he believed was ruining the American fabric. Billy Ray pulled into the garage, took a deep breath, turned his truck off and went inside. He was tired and hungry and wanted to see his son.

Chapter 18

FACING MY KIN

"Hey sweetie—what you doing?"

"Hey, baby, I'm headed to Target—wanna come?"

"Sure, you want me to come get you?"

"Yeah, that would be nice."

Larry loved his girlfriend. Even though she didn't approve of the way he treated black people, he knew she loved him too.

"Soooo—are you happy to be home for the break?"

"Yeah, I think so."

"You think so?"

"Yeah—I mean, I miss you and all, but…" Larry hesitated.

"But—O.K., baby, what's on your mind?"

Larry hadn't told anyone of his trip back to the 1800s because he knew no one would believe him. He didn't think his girlfriend, the one who he believed had his back in every situation, would believe him, or the fact that the experience had changed him. "Baby we will talk about it later."

"O.K."

The drive to Target was about a ten minute drive off of highway 32. Although McCormick was still about 50 years behind time, the community leaders like Billy Ray and the rest of the Order knew they weren't going to stop economic growth. Strip malls were replacing mom and pop stores it seemed like every few months—and Target was one of its prized community accomplishments.

Larry parked in Target's parking lot and he and his girlfriend went inside. He noticed all the cashiers were black and the managers were white. It reminded him of his recent trip. He and Sue walked around for a little bit looking at things.

"Hey baby, I'm gonna try on this shirt I like."

"OK—cool—I'll be over here at the electronics department."

"OK."

Larry started over to the electronics department when his eyes got very wide. He thought he had seen a ghost. He saw Penny standing near the CD aisle looking at some music with a few of her friends.

The interesting thing that crossed his mind was he saw the family resemblance. Penny was busy running her mouth and didn't see Larry when he walked up to her.

"Hey, Penny."

Penny and her friends thought it was strange Larry would come up to her and start talking. Although blacks and whites were now attending school together, there still was some tension among the races. It wasn't bad in the sense that whites and blacks didn't get along, it was just that besides sports and other school activities, they really didn't have anything in common. So when Larry walked up to Penny and spoke, she and her friends thought it was strange.

Larry couldn't take it anymore. He had to say something to his sister. He walked up to her and said, "Penny—is it possible I can talk with you alone?"

Although Penny was a little reluctant, she said, "Sure."

"Penny—I know you feel strange standing here talking to me, or wondering what in the hell do I want with you—but I really need to talk with you in private."

Looking slightly at her friends, Penny said, "Sure that's fine. When do you want to talk?"

Larry looked at Penny, "Here is my number—could you call me one day this week when you get a chance?"

"Sure. What day?"

Larry eyes were still fixated on Penny, "It doesn't matter—I just need to talk to you about something that is really important." Larry sounded distressed, but looked pleased and it was showing all in his facial expression.

"Sure, Larry—I'll call you tomorrow."

Larry found his girlfriend still trying to decide what she wanted to purchase for her mother for Christmas. She asked Larry what he thought about a shirt she was holding. He said the shirt was fine, but he really wasn't paying any attention to the shirt; he was thinking of what and how he was going to explain to Penny she was his sister. Larry took Sue to Chili's restaurant, they made small talk and had a bite to eat for a few hours then he took her home. Once home, he gave her a kiss and told her he would talk with her later on that night.

Chapter 19

THE CONVERSATION

The next day, Larry's phone rang. His ring tone was a song from one of his favorite bands, Rascal Flatts, "Life is a Highway." Although it was a remake, he really liked the song so he used it as one of his many cell phone ring tones. He answered the phone, but didn't recognize the number.

"Hello."

"Hey Larry—this is Penny."

Taking a deep breath, Larry said, "Hi, Penny."

In a non-caring way, Penny said, "Well, you wanted me to call—so—I'm calling."

"Penny, there's something I need to tell you and I really need to tell you in person, so can you meet me at the weigh station off of highway 20?"

Larry didn't know how Penny would respond, but he didn't care. All he knew is he wanted to tell his sister everything he knew about their relationship.

"Sure."

"Please come alone."

Penny was cool with that but she made sure she told her best friend Larry wanted to see her and if she didn't come back within a few hours to come to the weigh station on highway 20. "Ok—I'll see you in about 20 minutes."

Larry got in his truck and started the fifteen minute drive to the Georgia-South Carolina weigh station off of highway 20.

When Penny drove up she saw Larry looking around, back and forth in his truck like he was very antsy to see her. It was almost creepy to see Larry like this. She pulled up beside Larry's truck and rolled her window down,

"Hey Larry—what's up?"

Larry, seeing her, rolled his window down and responded to her, "Hey, Penny. Do you want me to come over to your car—or do you want to sit in my truck?"

Penny wanted to feel like she was in control, so she said, "Let's just sit at one of the picnic benches."

Again, Larry didn't care; he just wanted to talk with her.

"So, Larry—what is so important that I had to drive 20 minutes away from home?"

Larry didn't waste any time.

"Penny what do you know about your father?"

With a distraught look on her face, Penny asked, "Why do you want to know about my father?"

"I might have some information about your father." Larry answered.

"So you know Tank is not my father?"

"I sure do—'cause I know who your father is." Larry said.

Penny couldn't believe what she was hearing. Trying to sound calm, she asked, "And—how do you know about my father?"

"Well first, tell me what you know about your biological father."

Just knowing what her mother told her, and not wanting to sound like she didn't know her real father she said, "Well—he was a solider from up north—why do you ask? Have you heard from him, or do you know him?"

Larry looked at Penny in disbelief. He couldn't understand why Ms. Val hadn't told her—but then he realized if she would have told her she wouldn't have believed it. In fact, no one would have believed it.

"Penny—I'm your brother" Before she could comment, he continued, "My dad, the man you guys call Mr. B, is your father."

After Larry told Penny this she became very quiet and starting shaking. She didn't say anything for what seemed like a lifetime and when she spoke the only thing she could say was, "Why are you doing this to me?" As she started crying.

"Penny, please don't cry." Larry said trying to console his sister.

She eventually calmed down enough to listen to everything Larry had to tell her. Larry told her about the rape and the cover-up. He even went as far as to lecture her about the south not accepting the idea a man like their father could do something like that with a woman of color, with or without her consent, or the idea anyone would believe a man like Mr. B was capable of doing such a horrible thing. But it was the south in the 90s and in the south the 90s seemed like the 20s—especially in McCormick.

Penny wanted to know why was Larry telling her that—so when she finally said something she asked Larry, "Why are you now telling me this? I practically grew up with you—and even though we didn't say much at school, I don't understand why now you want to tell me this shit." Penny was going through the seven steps of grief and she was now on step three—anger! "Larry, you know you hate black people—why would you tell me this shit?" she said, now raising her voice.

Larry told Penny, in addition to him telling her about her father, about his trip to the 1800s and how his mission was to change and expose his father, a man he once admired. He was going to tell everyone what type of creep he was. He also wanted to let her know from that day forward he was going to try to do everything in his power to be a better man and change. He told her about Professor Truman and the whole slavery experience.

Penny didn't know how to act, or respond to what Larry had just told her but she knew he was sincere in what he was saying, and it

171

must have been true because she was twenty minutes away from home talking to someone who she thought would be the last person in the world she would be talking to about her father—so why not a trip to slavery? Still trying to digest what Larry had just said, Penny asked Larry, "Now what?"

The next thing Larry did was ask Penny for a hug. He hugged her for what seemed like an hour. They talked a little more when they left each other they promised they would be there for one other.

Two hours had passed and Penny's cell was ringing. Penny texted her girlfriend and told her everything was O.K. and she would see her later. Larry and Penny talked about another hour and just as they met, they left—both having a better perspective about each other, but more importantly, realizing they were family, and they both were cool with that.

Chapter 20

IT'S OK MOMMA, I LOVE YOU

Still a little devastated and confused, Penny had many things

going on in her head. She didn't want to tell her momma what she

had found out, but she didn't know whether to be upset at her mom

for not telling her the truth about her biological dad, or feel hopeless

about the horrific tragedy her mom must have endured when she was

being raped as a young teenage girl. One thing was a fact, she hated

her dad and thought of him as a monster, but she also knew he was

the most revered man in town, the state of South Carolina, or even

the world. All she could do is cry and wonder why. She didn't even

have the nerve to tell her closest friend Tamika. She knew she had

to confront her mom and she didn't know how to go about doing it.

Another thing that was crossing her mind was her step-dad. She

knew if Tank knew what had happened he would have killed Billy

Ray in his tracks—DEAD!

173

Penny thought about what she had to do for about a week and when she finally decided to tell Val, she was ready. "Mom—we need to talk."

Val knew when her daughter said mom the way she said it she was serious.

"Ok baby—when do you think we should have this conversation?"

Val sounded professional and kind of knew Penny was going to ask her the daddy questions again. What Val didn't know and was about to find out was going to change everything she knew about the old cliché "What you do in the dark, will come out in the light!"

"Mom, can we talk now?" Penny knew the timing was good because they were the only two at the house.

"Sure baby, what's on your mind?"

Penny didn't hesitate and just blurted it out. "I talked with my brother about a week ago."

Val was kind of confused at first because she thought Penny was talking about her little brother Dwayne. Not trying to look dumbfounded Val responded.

174

"And?"

"And I found out Billy Ray is my dad."

Val looked as if she had seen a ghost. She started hyperventilating and gasping for air. She started reliving the rape all over again in her mind, and the idea that her daughter was dropping this bombshell was almost unbearable.

"How—how did you…"

"I told you I talked to Bubba."

Val heard her say she talked to her brother but had no idea she was talking about her half-white-brother. "Oh—MY—God!"

"Why…" Her mind was racing and she was thinking, "Why would Bubba tell her this? How did Bubba know about this?" she said panicking.

"Momma—I love you!"

Chapter 21

THE CONFRONTATION

Bubba had been home only a few days. His avoidance of his

father was important because he wanted to confront his dad with

everything he knew about his sister, the Order and his newfound

ideology of human rights. He loved his dad but he also knew his dad

had a way of trying to make him feel like anything he did was best

for the family. Bubba knew in order for him to complete his cycle

against racial injustice, he had to confront the main source that drove

him to the way he viewed the world—his dad.

"Son have you been avoiding me for a reason?"

"No, sir, but I do want to ask you something."

"What's on your mind?"

"Dad, I love you—and I know you love me. But I can't continue

to live my life in a lie anymore." The more Bubba talked the louder

it seemed his voice got. "I am a recovering addict."

176

His dad looked at him with concern and with an expression that he had failed his son. Billy Ray truly thought Bubba was on drugs.

"Son—I didn't know."

"Dad—I'm not on drugs."

Billy Ray looked confused. "Whaaat-"

Before Billy Ray could say another word, Bubba said, "I'm not on drugs and never have been, or even had a desire to do drugs." Billy Ray sighed with a sound of relief—but after what came next, you would have thought he gave Billy Ray an aneurysm that would have killed him on the spot.

"Dad, what I'm recovering from is a severe case of racism! I'm a racist! You are a racist! And everyone in my world and yours are a bunch of racist bigots!"

"Boy—be careful for what you about to say!"

"No, dad—FUCK THAT! FUCK BEING CAREFUL! You and this whole town is nothing but a lie and I'm gonna expose all of you! I know everything—from you raping Ms. Val, to my sister Penny, from millions of dollars you have embezzled!"

"Now son wait just one GOT-DAM-MINUTE!"

"No—Dad, you wait a minute! So now you gonna kill me because I know the truth?" Bubba was so upset he started salivating at the mouth. Although he revered his dad, his anger trumped his fear. His dad tried to put his hand on his shoulder.

"Take your fucking hands off of me!"

Billy Ray was trying to tell Bubba to settle down to no avail. Billy Ray opened the drawer by the fireplace to take out a handkerchief to give to his weeping and upset son but acting out of fear that his dad was going to hurt him, Bubba picked up a black tool rod and struck his dad in the temple with the sharp potter tip end of the rod. Billy Ray fell from the blow but could have survived. When he fell, however the same temple that Bubba struck hit the sharp edge of their cement fireplace, killing him instantly.

Bubba's mother heard all the racket and the yelling and when she went to the study to see what was going on, she saw Bubba standing over his dad with a rod in his hand while his dad was lying on the floor bleeding profusely, not moving, with his eyes open and a handkerchief in his hand. She knew Billy Ray was dead. Bubba didn't quite understand what had just happened. He was in shock.

178

"Bubba—what have you done?"

"Mom—I—I—I. . . ."

"Oh my God—he's dead."

Although Mrs. Dixon was a quiet and reserved woman, she also was a very smart and catering mother to her children and husband. She was an old school carpetbagger Christian woman who had moved to the south shortly after she finished college in the most liberal state in the union—Boston, Massachusetts.

Tammy Tucker-Dixon came from a household which believed all men should be treated equal. So when she reluctantly dated and eventually gave into marrying Billy Ray, everyone was surprised. Especially her family who never caught on to the idea their daughter was marrying a self-centered bigot. I think in some way Tammy believed she could change Billy Ray, but with his strong "Type A-personality" and manipulation of everyone he came into contact with, she realized he was a lost soul. In her prison, she did what she thought would be best for her and the kids—be quiet, be humble, raise her family the best she could, and stay out of her husband's way.

179

So when she was faced with the dilemma of what to do when she came across her son standing over her husband, she didn't waver. She knew her husband and she knew her son. Although she wasn't aware of the newfound redemption her son's trip to Willie Lynch's hell had wrought, she knew in any case, she was going to do what it took to save her son. When Bubba calmed down, he explained to her what happened. She told him to go take a nice hot bath and let her deal with it.

Chapter 22

THE TRUTH WILL SET YOU FREE

"9-1-1 emergency, what is your emergency?"

Tammy knew she had to say the right thing so there would be no room for error.

"My name is Tammy Dixon and my husband fell and hit his head and is not breathing!"

"Ma'am, are you alone?"

"No—my son is here, but he is upstairs, I think in the bathroom."

"OK, ma'am, we are sending the ambulance and the police right away."

"Thank you!" Tammy said sounding frantic over the phone. She knew if she was going to pull this off with any question, she had to be spot on in how she addressed the Emergency Service dispatcher. Tammy was careful in what she touched. She could see Billy Ray had clearly hit his head on the edge side of the step up of the cement fireplace. She also noticed the fireplace rod lying next to Billy

181

Ray's body with a small bloodstain on it. She picked up the rod and put it in a place she knew only her and Jesus would find.

Chapter 23

WHAT'S NEXT

My cell phone rang about 9 p.m. I had just gotten home

from some Christmas shopping and was hungry. Although I took

Larry's number at the school and gave him mine I did like most

people, I forgot to record it in my cell database. So when the

unidentified number rang to the sound of Mozart 5th symphony, I

didn't know who it was.

"Hello."

"Dr. Truman!" A distressed voice was on the other in.

"Yes—this is he." Sounding real professional.

"This is Larry."

"Hey son—Merry Christmas." Although it was a few days from

Christmas, I figured it was the proper thing to say.

"I did it!" There were many things I could have thought of I

hoped Larry could and would have done. However, my mind was

just so at ease because he took the time to call, which I knew wouldn't be an easy task for him considering the traumatic experience he had at school.

"Did what, son?"

"I killed HIM!"

"Killed who, son?"

"I didn't mean to, but he's dead!" Larry was sounding so confused, I thought he was drunk.

"Larry—take your time son and tell me what's going on."

"I got into an argument with my dad and when he came at me I struck him in the head with a fireplace rod—he's dead."

"O.K., son...."

"They just came and got him and I'm home with my mother and sister."

I knew Larry needed me more than ever now and I wanted to make sure what I said next would not only ease his mind, but also help him through this horrible ordeal. Although Larry's dad was a bigot, he was still his father. I also felt I was in some small way responsible for Larry's actions. Larry had been changed. Change is

184

an incredible thing; most of the time when a person is faced with an incredible life-changing act, they don't know what to do. Change is a learned and experienced process. We start this process as soon as we leave the comforts of our mother's womb.

However, the change Larry was experiencing was a different type of change. We must remember, most change comes at a slow and methodical pace. However, when you experience a process of change the way Larry experienced, the body tries to protect itself with defense mechanisms to keep it sane. In Larry's case, I gave him a gift, which led to the process of change on steroids. His change was like being on a drug like heroin and going cold turkey without any professional help or support from family, or friends, which could literally have killed him. So it was important I helped Larry through this process.

Since it was close to Christmas and this was the time for love, cheer and a deference for the fellow man, I thought it would be important we got together after the holiday so we could really deal with this horrible tragedy.

185

"Larry, I need you to be calm and know you are a smart and good young man. Whatever you have done I know it was done out of fear and you protecting yourself from a horrible situation."

He agreed and calmed down.

"I want you to spend some time with your family and when you guys decide to bury your dad, let me know—I want you to come back to school early so you and I can spend some time together, and you don't have to stay on campus, you can stay with me and my family."

"Yes, sir."

Chapter 24

THE FUNERAL

Billy Ray's funeral was somber and sad. Many dignitaries

from around the state and country were there showing their support

for what many knew as a great businessman and patriot. Most of the

businesses in town were closed for the funeral. Even the governor

allowed the city to go half-staff for this desolate event. Although

Billy Ray was a bigot, he was a hero to many of the townspeople and

business owners around South Carolina, the United States and

internationally. Many African-Americans paid reverence to who

they thought was their savior. Remember, Billy Ray employed

many blacks in McCormick, so in their minds, he was a good and

fair man. Larry couldn't believe the masses of people that showed

up to his dad's funeral, especially the African-American community.

He saw African-Americans sobbing as if they knew him personally,

like a close friend or relative.

The Lutheran of Our Lord was at capacity. There were over 2,000 people there and about a few thousand outside. You would have thought Elvis had died. The city contributed a whole day to broadcasting the funeral on television. It was like the Macy's Thanksgiving Day Parade with the local announcers getting their fifteen minutes of fame, announcing the important people who had come to town for the funeral. From the governor to the local NAACP—everyone was there. That's right—the NAACP. Billy Ray was a big donor to the NAACP, and without his support the local chapter couldn't stay afloat. This is what Billy Ray was trying to teach his son about how to keep the blacks in their place—keep them close, somewhat employed, and confused.

Larry was tired, frustrated and sad. He never intended on hurting his father, not to the point of killing him. He just wanted him to stop being such a horrible person, especially to the people who were making his many businesses thrive for almost a generation. Larry didn't understand how the people he had once revered were the people who were instrumental to the success of his family's fortune, but he knew his dad was the ultimate manipulator—a true wolf in sheep clothing. Another thing Larry learned was these same people

he once hated were loyal to a man whom he would eventually

accidently kill—and that's why the outcry was so devastating to a lot

of the African-Americans in the area. They acted as if it were JFK or

Martin Luther King's assassinations. Larry thought for a moment,

"Why do these people love my dad so much when he treated them

like shit?" That thought would resonate with Larry until he had a

chance to get back to school and ask Dr. Truman.

Christmas was a little strange at the Dixons, but they all got

through it. Larry did get a chance to spend some time with his

girlfriend and sister. He would eventually tell his girlfriend about

his sister and the experience he had had while at school. Although

she was surprised and a little skeptical about what he was saying, she

was very excited that the new Larry, the man she loved, wasn't

going down the same road of hatred and bigotry that killed his

father. Because the family was loved throughout the community,

after the investigation, the death of his father was ruled as an

accident. About a week before school started back, Larry decided to

get a head start so he could put his head around all the events that had taken place. It was shortly after the New Year's and about a few weeks after the death of his father. Larry explained to his mother he would be leaving a little early because he had something to do. So a week before school, he decided to call Dr. Truman and take him up on his offer.

Chapter 25

THE GIVER

Larry left for school after the holidays. His time home was

bittersweet. He enjoyed spending time with his family and Penny

and learned they had more in common than he realized. He left for

school early on a Sunday morning but before he left he had breakfast

with her at the Waffle House near the interstate. They talked about

many things especially bridging the gap between siblings. Larry

knew the only people who knew about his half-sister were his

girlfriend, Ms. Val, God and his deceased dad. He also knew he

would have to eventually tell his mom and the rest of the world.

Larry talked with Penny a few more hours and with a few more

salutations, hugs, and I love yous, he was on his way back to school.

The last vision he had before he left was his sister smiling and

waving good-bye.

Larry thought about his dad and his mother on his long trip back. He often thought about what drove them to a great life, but a horrible life of bigotry. He thought of a mother who was very smart and sweet, but was driven by her weak constitution to please a man who was pure evil. He thought about all the millions of people around the world, black and white, who suffered from hating one another for no apparent reason other than the color of one's skin. Larry arrived at the Alabama state line mid evening. Before he knew it, he was about a good hour from my house.

Although he was reluctant to come stay with my family he was excited he had a chance to reunite with the person who had changed his life. Larry got to my house a little after six in the evening. We were about to sit down for dinner, so his timing was perfect. My wife and I greeted Larry in the driveway. I introduced him to my wife and my silly dog Jasmine, who started investigating this new person who had just pulled into our driveway. Jasmine investigated Larry as if he was a runaway prisoner. She gave us her approval by looking up at me and Sara and waving her tail profusely.

"Hey, Larry—how was your trip here?"

192

"It was a good trip."

"Well, come on in—we were about to have dinner."

"Hey, girl." Jasmine loved it when someone showed her attention and Larry poured it on. After a few minutes of loving on Jasmine, Larry grabbed his suitcase and came inside.

"Baby, I think Jasmine has found a suitor."

"I love dogs—my da-" Larry started to express he and his dad had hunting dogs.

"It's okay, son—come on in."

"Larry, let me show you to your room and show you where you can freshen up for dinner."

"Thanks, Mrs. Dixon."

"Oh, honey—don't call me Mrs. Dixon, that would be Truman's mother." They both started laughing. "You can call me Sara or Sam."

"Larry—you are not upstairs trying to steal my wife are you."

"No, sir." he replied, laughing.

Larry went into the bathroom to freshen up and Sara came back downstairs.

"What a sweet young man."

Dinner was like any other dinner. Larry was thinking, "Man, this reminds me of the family dinners we use to have back home." Before we sat down for dinner, I took Larry for a quick tour of the house. We stopped by the study, or what Sara would call "the Cave." The first thing Larry noticed were the many books I had in the study. I had books from ancient Greek mythology to the Bible. Larry also noticed many magazines, he also thought he even saw a few comic books. The thing that caught his attention the most, were the many pictures I had in the study. Larry stared at the photos and saw many pictures of my youth.

He noticed I was always smiling. Larry thought for a minute, "WOW! The professor must love his family."

Sara yelled out, "Come get it, boys!"

"Larry, have a seat. Hope you like fried chicken?"

"Yes, ma-" He started to say ma'am, but remembered what she told him a few minutes earlier. "Yes, I love fried chicken."

"Larry, don't let my beautiful wife fool you—she is a dynamic cook."

194

Larry thought, "The Truman's really love each other, they act like high school kids in love." Larry just watched how they interacted with each other, smiled and continued with small talk around the table until dinner was finished. In his mind, Larry also thought Dr. Truman was correct in his assessment about the beauty of his wife and her cooking skills. "Dear, Mr. Dixon and I are heading to the Cave."

"O.K. honey. Larry, don't let him start telling you about his days in high school." Sara knew if I started talking about those years, I would keep him in the cave for hours—or even days, but that's not why we went to the cave.

He just laughed and politely said, "I won't."

Chapter 26

FIGURING IT OUT

"So, Larry, what is your plan?" I knew Larry really wanted to

figure out how to deal with everything he had just experienced in

just a short time.

Larry thought about his journey to the 1800s. He thought about

his hero, Willie Lynch. He thought about his half-sister Penny. He

thought about the death of his dad and more importantly, he thought

about making a change for the better.

"Well, Dr. Truman, I kinda know what I want to do. I truly want

to finish school, however, since you are allowing me to deal with my

issues, I think I will go back home and make things right."

I didn't quit understand what Larry meant about making things

right, but I knew Larry was smart enough that he would have

thought about how he wanted to make things right. All I wanted to

know is whether Larry was really ready to face the outcome. "So,

Larry are you ready to deal with everything that will happen when you mix things up at home?"

"I don't think I would ever be ready, but if I'm going to do this, I better do it while it's fresh in my mind."

"When are you planning to return home?"

"Well, since I talked with you, I figured it will be best if I leave tomorrow morning."

"O.K., then. Get some rest and we will talk a little bit more tomorrow before you leave in the morning."

"Yes, sir."

Larry said his good nights to me and Mrs. Truman, petted Jasmine on the head and went into the room that was prepared for him. He slightly closed the door after he dressed for bed and as he was lying in bed, Jasmine came in and stood by the bed on the side Larry was preparing to sleep on. Larry had closed his eyes when he felt he was being watched by someone, or something. He opened his eyes and saw Jasmine looking at him, wagging her tail and panting.

"Hey girl—you staying in here with me tonight?" When Jasmine heard Larry's voice, she sat down and gave her paw to Larry. "O.K., girl—I see you, I'm here!" Larry said grabbing Jasmine's paw, and rubbed her on the head for a few minutes. After the little courtship between the two new friends, Jasmine walked to the door, looked back at Larry and lay down by the door as if she was guarding Larry from the boogieman. Larry also thought, "I guess Jasmine is letting me know she also supports my decision." With that, Larry was off to sleep.

Chapter 27

MAKING IT RIGHT

Larry rose early the next morning. He really didn't have to worry about packing because he was at my house less than 24 hours before he was to make the trip back home. Larry wanted to leave before anyone woke, because he didn't want to wake them. However, they were early risers themselves. When Larry got himself together and headed downstairs, he ran into Sara dressed in her workout clothes.

"Good morning, Larry."

"Good morning, Sara."

"Truman told me you were leaving this morning and I wanted to see you before you left. Come on in the kitchen and let me make you something to eat before you hit the road. Truman should be down shortly."

Larry and Sara were in the kitchen having small talk while she was cooking breakfast. Larry told Sara about his experience with Jasmine and they both burst out with laughter. As she was putting a pot on the stove to cook some grits, I came downstairs.

"I heard you guys laughing—Larry, you are a smooth operator. You trying to steal my favorite girl?"

Although I was very smart, my humor was dry. When I get a laugh from a joke I had once told, I will tell it over and over again until it losses its luster. The, "you trying to steal my girl?" joke was funny the first time, but it only got a semi-laugh the second time. It even looked like Jasmine was shaking her head as to say, "Come on Truman."

Larry, wanting to amuse me, laughed anyway. "No, sir, Dr. T— I wasn't trying to steal your best girl."

"I got my eye on you, son." We all laughed—it even looked like Jasmine was laughing.

"Well Larry, I want you to have a great trip home and you need to keep me posted on your plans."

"Yes, sir." We finished breakfast, talked a little more, said our goodbyes, and Larry started back home.

Chapter 28

BACK HOME AGAIN

The ride home was a little easier than it was the first time he left for the Christmas break. Larry was at peace and he knew what he wanted to do. Larry got home about mid-afternoon.

"Hey, baby, you back from school already?"

"Yeah, mother, Dr. Truman gave me a reprieve because I told him I had to tie up some loose ends."

"Sure, sweetie, is there anything I can do?"

"Mother, is there anyway, or do you have the keys to dad's safe deposit box at the bank?"

"Yes—but why in the world you want to get in dad's bank box?"

"I remember dad telling me there was something in it I will eventually need." Because of Billy Ray's unexpected death, no one really knew what was in his deposit box.

Billy Ray was very careful about the business of the Order. There were only a few people in the state that knew all the improprieties that drove the Order to the prominence it was. Billy Ray was the Order and he only entrusted a few people with all of the biddings of the Order. Now there were a few people like the Governor, a few senators and some of the business people who had some information about the Order. However, the information they had was peanuts and only painted a small picture of what the Order was truly about. Larry knew in order to get the damning information he needed to sabotage the Order, he needed to get into his father's safe deposit box. Because of the secrecy of the Order, Billy Ray was smart enough to safe guard the entire puzzle of his empire to only him and his up and coming protégé, his son Larry. The problem with such limited knowledge to a select few was, Billy Ray was dead and the one person he trusted the most was now about to go rogue.

Tammy wasn't really sure where her husband kept the key to his safe deposit box, but after his death she gathered up most of his things and stored them in the basement. So when Larry asked her about the keys to the safe deposit box, she assumed the keys would, or must be with the rest of his stuff that she was keeping for sentimental value. "Larry, I stored all of your dad's stuff in the basement. If you check in one of the boxes you should find keys for his safe deposit box."

"Thanks, mother."

Larry wasted no time. He searched a few boxes and found a box that was labeled miscellaneous/ keys and started looking for the keys in that box. Larry thought to himself, "Damn, Dad, why all the keys? Wait a minute, what am I thinking? I know McCormick is a little late with technology, but I don't need a key."

Tammy came down to the basement as to help Larry look for the keys. Realizing he didn't need a key, he told his mom he found it to keep her from worrying. "Thanks mother—I'll see you in a few hours."

"Hello, Mr. Dixon, welcome to McCormick National Bank, how may I assist you?"

"Is Mr. Steward here?" Mr. Steward was the bank manager.

"Yes—just a minute—was he expecting you?"

Freddie Gavin

"No, but I wanted to ask him something." Because everyone

knew the Dixons and Billy Ray's influence in the community, Larry

knew once his name was mentioned, Mr. Steward would come out of

his office ready to kiss Larry's ass as if he was the President of the

United States.

"Mr. Dixon, How may I help you? I am so sorry for your loss."

"Thank you, Mr. Steward, I was wondering if I was authorized to

get the contents out of my father's safe deposit box?"

"Come to my office, Mr. Dixon, and let me check." Mr. Steward

was a tall thin man. He wore thick glasses and was the most

professional guy within a thousand miles. Larry knew if his name

was on the safe deposit box, Steward would let him in, give him the

key and privacy—nothing asked. Steward was not only a

professional, he was also by the book.

Mr. Steward checked his records. "Hum—let's see—um—

O.K.—yes, Mr. Dixon, you are the sole proprietor of your father's

safe deposit box. Follow me please." Mr. Steward escorted Larry

into a secured room in the back, gave him the key to box 1024, and left the room. "Mr. Dixon, when you are ready to leave, please pick up the red phone on the desk—have a nice day."

"Thanks, Mr. Steward."

"You are truly welcome."

Chapter 29

WOW

Larry remembered reading an article from Business Pundit that read, "They may sit behind marble desks, wearing expensive suits, with their ties done up to 11 o' clock – but that doesn't mean they won't… steal your cash?"   The Order was a huge operation by most accounts. Its businesses endeavors grew from a small town in South Carolina to be one of America's 7th largest organizations, employing 21,000 staff in more than 40 countries. Larry knew the success of The Order's firm turned out to be an elaborate scam. Through the use of accounting loopholes, special purpose entities and poor financial reporting, senior executives were able to hide billions in debt from failed deals and projects. Among the firm's crimes were: manipulating power markets, bribing foreign governments to win contracts abroad, and manipulating the energy market.

Larry knew this because he now had all the information he needed to ruin the Order. One visit to the bank and a little technology device we now take for granted, was the culprit to his reign of exposure. The "Thumb Drive." A little device that would eventually be the hallmark for how we store and keep information safe would be the demise of the Order. Small in size, but big in force—not the force we see when a large hurricane or tornado destroy our towns and cities—but a force that when in the right hands, could destroy states and possible small countries. This force was now in the hands of a young smart recovering racist who wanted to make things right for the same people whose lives were destroyed over 400 years ago. A people whom he thought he hated. A people he knew were exploited by some of these scams. He wanted to make things right, especially to the many African-Americans whom he knew he had wronged, but more importantly, he wanted to make it right for his sister who he now had an affection and an everlasting love for.

Larry researched his plan of destruction. He wanted to make sure when he destroyed his dad's businesses, it wouldn't affect his family fortunes. Although his plan would also be dangerous, he knew he had to protect his biological sister and his mother. Once he knew his mother and sister were clear from harm and financial devastation, he put his plan in action.

"Ring, ring, ring."

"Thank you for calling CNN, if you know your party's extension please dial it or say it-"

"What the FUCK?" Larry said, "I hate these damn automation calls. Do people even answer phones anymore?"

Although a little frustrated, Larry knew exactly what to do.

"Hello, Dr. Truman?"

"Yes—is this Larry?"

"Yes, sir."

"How are you doing son—it's been about a month since I heard from you?"

"I'm doing well but I do have a question."

Although Larry told me most things, he wasn't going to tell me anything about the plan he had in place until it was fully exposed on national T.V. Like a concerned father I asked, "What's your question son?"

"I was wondering, could you, or do you know someone from CNN I can talk with and give something to?"

I knew many people. I also knew one of CNN's best news anchors personally, Don Lemon. I met Don several years ago when he was an anchor for WBRC in Birmingham, Alabama. We would also see each other at conferences around the U.S. So when Larry needed someone to talk with, I knew exactly who to call.

"Sure, Larry. Give me a day to contact a friend of mine at CNN and he will be getting back to you soon. So have you figured things out yet?"

"Yes sir, I will be getting back in touch with you soon. Tell your lovely wife and my girl Jasmine I said hello."

"I sure would, and I'll talk with you soon."

Little did I know, once Larry talked with Mr. Lemon, the sooner would be before I could digest our recent conversation.

Chapter 30

EXPOSURE

"Hello, this is Don Lemon of CNN news."

"Hello Mr. Lemon, I was told by one of my professors, Dr. Truman, you would call me back."

"Yes, indeed, son—Truman is a dear friend of mine, and who doesn't love his wife Sara."

"Yeah, he accused me of trying to steal her from him." Both men burst out with laughter.

"So, how can I help you?"

"Well, Mr. Lemon."

"Call me Don."

"Don, are you familiar with OTOCH Corporations?"

"Is that the one that's own by Mr. Dixon?"

"Yes—I'm his son Larry."

Don said Mr. Dixon as if he didn't know who Larry was, but he knew the story from me.

211

"First, let me give you my condolences to you and your family."

"Thanks, Don. Well, I have some information I think would be newsworthy…"

"Go ahead…"

"I have information, if leaked could destroy the operations of OTOCH industries."

"Larry, I'm going to assume you do have this information." He said. "I'm also going to assume the information you have could put you in grave danger."

I think we should meet in person and you bring me what you think I should have. This would also, be the safest way to expedite the information you have."

"Yes sir—so what day, or when do you want to get together?"

Don knew this information was going to expose billions of dollars in assets, so he really wanted to protect the interest of all parties.

"How about I meet you in Columbia, South Carolina, Sunday morning."

"Sure—that's fine."

"I'll give you the address, give me a day or two to talk with my boss and I'll let you know where to meet me."

"Thanks Don, and I promise you will not be disappointed."

Chapter 31

THE MEETING

Larry left home about 4 am for the short drive to Columbia,

South Carolina. He knew this meeting was going to be an important

meeting with one of America's premier cable network news

personalities. He arrived at the Double Tree hotel that was close by

the university around 6:15 am. Larry sat in his car waiting to hear

from Don.

"Ring, Ring." Larry looked at his phone and thought why Don

would be calling him from the state of Utah.

"Hello!"

"Hello, is this Mr. Dixon!"

"Yes."

"We have an offer…"

Before the guy on the other end with the foreign accent could

finish, Larry hung up the phone. Larry thought to himself, "I am so sick in tired of these dang teller marketers calling my cell—how in the hell did they get my number."

The phone rang again and Larry was a little reluctant to answer if he didn't recognize a number that had an area code that was familiar. The area code was 404. Larry knew that was a Georgia area code because he had family that lived in the neighboring state. "Hello…"

"Mr. Dixon." Don said Larry's name like they had been friends since grade school.

"Hello Don."

"Larry, if you are here, come on up, I am in room triple 7."

"Knock, knock." Don opened the door.

"Hello, Larry."

Larry noticed immediately Don was very friendly, but very professional. He was dressed in jeans and a white collared shirt with a pair of black dress shoes. Don was a medium-skinned African-American. He had a nicely trimmed haircut and a pair of glasses on his head as if he had just been reading. "Would you like anything to drink?"

"No, thank you."

"So, Mr. Dixon, what's behind your exposure of one of the most successful companies in America?"

"Well, Don, I was bamboozled. Everything I learned from a man and group I held in high regards was a lie."

Without getting to his experience to the 1800s, he talked about race, his sister, the Order, and his old way of thinking.

He expressed his love for his mother, but he also knew she played a small part in the way he thought. Larry was angry. Don patiently listened and recorded everything Larry said on one of those small voice recorders. Larry left Don with the thumb drive that had all the incriminating information about his father's company.

"Larry, you realize once I publicize this information your life will not be the same?"

"I understand, and because of how ruthless the guys in my father's company are, I will want to go on your show and talk about my father's company."

"Well, I also would like you to contact the FBI."

"Why?"

"Because you will need protection from all the backlash."

216

Larry, thought about what Don had said. He agreed to everything and all the advice Don had given him, even the part about receiving FBI protection. A few more hours of talking about the improprieties of his father's company and Larry was eager to get back home.

After his meeting with Don Lemon, Larry felt like he had just had a huge burden lifted off of his shoulders. He didn't care about the outcome of the exposure, the Order, FBI, no one. Larry was at peace. He often reflected on my words and advice. He thought about his mom and sister and his new addition to his family, his half-sister Penny.

"Well, Mr. Dixon, when I get the story together, I will be contacting you on a release day and a date to come on my show."

And as quickly as they had met, Larry had left Columbia and was on his way back to McCormick.

Chapter 32

BREAKING NEWS

CNN was not one of those channels Larry was becoming used to

watching. He was a FOX News guy for most of his life. However,

he knew today would be a special day for him. CNN was a liberal

news channel that was great about flashing "Breaking News" across

the television screen even if the news wasn't newsworthy. However,

they knew when they flashed their breaking news billboard on the

T.V. screen, the propaganda wheel would take over from there,

causing everyone who was watching CNN, or anyone who just had

their televisions on the CNN channel to stop what they were doing

and focus on this so called "Breaking News."

Larry didn't say anything to anyone about what was about to

change his and his family's lives for good. Larry had talked with

Don and gave him the damaging information about his father's

company about two months prior. About a week before the story was

218

supposed to air, he traveled to Atlanta and did a pre-recorded piece about his father's company.

Don did his research. He wanted to maximize the story of The OTOCH Organization and all the business ventures. He knew when OTOCH was exposed it would cripple the organization and send people to jail for no less than a century. It was all about timing and Don knew it.

The FBI contacted Larry a few days after the Columbia meeting. Don had a contact in the FBI and his contact made sure he handled the process of information Don had sent him very delicately. For about a month, it was becoming a little strange around the McCormick area. Everything was hushed. Although Larry was aware of the FBI's presence, the community wasn't aware of their presence nor did they know why these strange men in black suits were hanging out in McCormick. However, the community did wonder why the main office of OTOCH was taped off and all of the 48 employees in the building were put on paid leave without any explanation. Most people in or around the small town in South

Carolina just assumed the taped-off building was done this way for repairs.

There were talks about repairing some of the infrastructure. Rumors ran rampant but no one really knew what was happening. The only people who knew were Larry, Don Lemon, most of the OTOCH board members--who were scared--and the FBI. So when Larry was sitting in his father's study getting ready to watch Don Lemon's "Breaking News" story, he was excited, a little skeptical, scared and antsy. He knew he would be the one to bring down this billion-dollar good ole boys society, called the Order, all disguised by OTOCH Corporations.

Advertising had run all month on the OTOCH organization. Don's prompted a must–see story about the OTOCH Corporation while he did his midday daily show on CNN. He used words like 'a must–see story of love and hate,' damning words like racism, greed, and scam. And statements like, "Not since ENRON has it ever been such a scandal." He made references in comparison to Watergate and even found a way to call the leader of the organization Al Capone.

In other words, the shit was about to hit the fan and Don was leading the charge.

Don Lemon's story aired late evening and he did the whole piece about the OTOCH Corporation. The piece lasted about two hours with commercials. The producer, Randy Coffer, organized the piece so at the end of all the history, personal history and personnel who were involved in the organization's executive board, there would be a 15-minute interview with Don and the whistleblower, and son of the ringleader, Larry.

The piece was devastating. Everyone who was important in the OTOCH organization were exposed. Don exposed the Order and the racist practices; he exposed all the mounds of information he received from Larry. He built a type of rags to riches story about Larry's father. He talked about how he started from nothing and would eventually have the ear of world leaders. He connected the Order, led by Larry's father, and drew the merit of big money, greed, political influence, while tying it all to his hatred of Jews, blacks and anyone who wasn't considered Anglo-Saxon. The bottom line of Don's breaking news story was that OTOCH Corporation was a billion-dollar organization and their leader, Mr. Dixon, was a horrible man. He was a very smart and cunning man, however, a true devil on earth in **practically plan sight.**

The last part of the interview was a sit down with Don and Larry, the son of the devil. The smart young man who thought his daddy was a God would eventually learn, even though he loved his daddy, he was a horrible manipulating man. Don and Larry talked about Larry attending college and meeting Professor Truman. Although he didn't get into how Dr. Truman changed his life magically, he did explain to Don if it wasn't for Dr. Truman, he would have got caught up like his father did, which he believed would continue the ugly cycle of greed and hatred. He did tell Don he was a recovering racist and was in love with the idea of Willie Lynch.

"Yes, Don, I put myself, with the help of Dr. Truman, on a million step program of recovery."

"Why do you call it a million step program?"

"Well I figured since a young age, racism has always been a part of my fabric—it defined me. It has been a systemic part of my soul." he explained.

222

He explained how Dr. Truman showed him a different perspective of what racism was all about, which he believed was instrumental in helping him transform into the person he was that day. They talked about his family—all of his family, which included his half-sister Penny who he had recently met. He explained how beautiful and kind she was and how he and she had a great relationship.

The two-hour breaking news piece by Don Lemon achieved some of the highest ratings of any program recently aired—over 10 million viewed. The request for the re-airing for the many patrons who didn't see it was overwhelming.

Don's piece aired for the whole month. By the time the last airing of the "OTOCH V. Order" had ended, Larry had become some type of folk celebrity. People were calling him the "change maker." He even went on several radio talk and television shows talking about his father's organization and how racism once influenced his thinking.

Although at times things seemed a little overwhelming, Larry knew once he had opened Pandora's box, he would be in for the long

223

haul. He embraced his new position and stayed in constant contact with Dr. Truman.

Chapter 33

IT'S OVER

"Hey Penny, what are you doing?"

"Hey bro—getting ready to do what I always do on a beautiful cold Saturday—go hang with some friends and grab some lunch. You want to come?"

"Nooooo—I do not want to hang with you and your crazy girlfriends." They both burst out with laughter.

"Yeah, Tamika thinks you are hot for a white boy." They start laughing again.

"What's up?"

"Well, I have something for you. Ms. Val and the family and was wondering, could I come by later?"

"Sure."

"Let's say about 7?"

"That would be nice."

"Ok, see you at 7." Larry was a little anxious about going to Tank and Val's house to visit his sister, but he knew he had to.

Larry didn't do much that day. He just hung around the house, talked with his mom and spoke to his girlfriend on the phone. They texted back and forth about college and life. She was wondering when he was going to go back. He told her something he hadn't told her about what I had told him. "Yeah sweetie, with all the things that were going on, Dr. Truman got permission from the school administration for me to be able to take a break until next semester. He asked me to just write a paper and keep him informed and it would be O.K."

"That's awesome."

"Yeah."

"You really like Dr. Truman don't you?"

"Yeah, he's cool and I know you would like him too."

Time had passed and it was getting close to seven. "O.K. honey, I'll talk with you later."

"O.K. Larry."

Larry took a quick shower. While in the shower he got his thoughts together. After all the time he had spent with his sister Penny, he had never visited her at her home. He knew Ms. Val and the legendary Tank, but he never formally met neither of them.

About seven o'clock, Larry arrived at his sister's house. Penny lived with her parents on what is considered the black side of town—modest low-income homes—across the railroad tracks. Most families had an average income of about eighteen dollars a year. Most homes were owned by, you guess it, OTOCH Corporation. This was considered a very small percentage of the OTOCH organization, about 00.0001 percent to be exact. I think Mr. Dixon owned most of these homes, not because it was a great investment, but more so because owning them meant he owned most of the community, and some of the patrons had been living there for over 40 years. Larry thought to himself, "Damn, my dad was a horrible man." These homes were built cheaply, were overpriced and most people would die before they could pay them off. Most of the homes were revolving doors—three to four generation homes. Although this area wasn't the best place to live, most of the residents took

227

pride in their overpriced abodes. The average home size was about 1,300 square feet—great for a starter home, or home for a young family of two. However, most of these homes had at least five or six people living in them. So when Larry got out of his car, he was kind of prepared for the overcrowded household. This was also the first time he had ever been in a home that his father owned and he only lived a few miles away.

"Knock, Knock." Larry knocked on the door and Penny came to the door. "Hey, bro!"

Excited, Larry responded and gave his sibling a big hug.

"Hey, sis!"

"Come on in."

"Hey, Ms. Val."

"Hey Larry—Tank went to the store and he should be back in a little bit."

"That's okay."

"I hadn't seen you in a while—not since the mess-"

Before she could complete her sentence, Larry cut her off, in a nice way to avoid talking about what she was referring—but it was a mess.

"Yeah—but you been doing okay?"

"Yes Larry, we are hanging in there."

"Hey baby." Tank had returned from the store.

"Hey, Mr. Tank."

Tank didn't like it when people tried to be so formal, but he didn't mind Larry calling him Mr. Tank.

"How you doing son?"

Everyone knew about the recent interview and destruction of the OTOCH Corporation, so you could hear it in Tank's voice when he spoke, he was being sympathetic to Larry's family recent issues.

The whole Thompson family, even the kids, gathered in the small living area. Larry talked about college—he even talked about Tank's early years and how he was revered on and off the football field. He respected Tank because he knew Tank was not a conformist, but a self-made man that loved his family.

229

"So I guess everyone wants to know why I wanted to come by—well, I hope everyone wants to know."

Larry talked about all the wrongs and injustices he saw as a young man. And even though Penny found out who her real father was, and the family had talked about it and moved passed it, he still wanted to apologize to Valarie for his late father's actions. Through a few tears in the living room, Valarie accepted his apology on behalf of his father. Even though it wasn't from Satan himself, Valarie and her family had moved past the incident and wanted Larry to move past it too, so she accepted his apology. He talked about being more of a brother to his sister and promised to visit more.

Larry pulled out a few envelopes he had in a little briefcase. He gave the first envelope to the kids in the sum of about five hundred thousand dollars. He explained to them he knew he came from wealth and he wanted, what he called his new brother and sisters, because of his sister Penny, to have the same opportunity he had as a child. "You guys should be able to go to a great college like I'm attending and I know you will do great things. And even if you

230

decide not to attend college, I hope this money will give you a good start." The check was a little overwhelming for everyone in the room—even Tank.

The second envelope he gave to his sister Penny. Penny opened the envelope and just stared.

"Oh my God!"

Larry had given her a check for two million dollars.

"Sis—do whatever you want to do—I'm glad I met you and I know we are truly related—I love you!"

Penny started crying, showed her mom the check, and embraced her brother for what seemed like forever. Without even breaking his hug from his sister, he handed Valarie an envelope. As she opened the envelope, Penny loosened her grip and sat in a chair that was brought from the kitchen to make sure everyone had a place to sit. Valarie opened the envelope but couldn't look at the amount—so she just handed it to Tank.

"Ms. Val, again, I know I could never repay you for what my father did to you. But in a way, I'm kinda glad of the incident because if not for that one horrible night, I wouldn't have met my

231

sister and all of you guys, so I'm very grateful for part of the story—

being my sister, Penny." Valarie still didn't know what was on the

check, because she was still a little overwhelmed over the first two

envelopes.

In the envelope, Tank noticed it was a list of names, a deed, and a

check. When Tank looked at the check, he couldn't believe his eyes.

"Twwwweeeennty mmmmiiillllion ddollaars!"

Tank fell back in his chair. Everyone thought Tank was going to

have a heart attack.

Before anyone could say anything, Larry said, "Let me explain

the list. First, Mr. Tank, the deed is for your home you now own—

secondly, the list of names is for all the residences in the area that

my dad once owned. I have made arrangements for everyone who

bought a home from my dad to get the deed to their home at no cost.

All homes are paid off and property taxes are paid off for the next

ten years—I want you guys to pass these deeds out as a late

Christmas gift from our family."

That night, even though the holiday had since passed, the

Thompson household was filled with holiday cheer, laughter, and gratitude. Larry knew although he had given his new family a great gift, it couldn't compare to the gift he received that evening while sitting in my office. A gift that freed him from total destruction of the mind—the gift of ridding him of hate.

Chapter 34

FICTION—But True

One night, I had a dream. This dream would eventually, over a

period of a year, turn into the story you have just read. The dream I

had was so vivid; I was compelled to write it down. No, I'm not a

writer and I never had a desire to write. As a student in high school

and college, I hated taking notes, so writing has never been my

thing, unless it was lyrics to a song. I am an educated 56-year-old,

African-American security professional with over thirty plus years of

experience. I am also a musician, which I love!

This book is a dream of my thoughts about the best and worst of

what I think of humanity. I believe I will always stand for, and pray

for what most human beings that exist on this place we call earth

desire for, true love in a society free of bigotry and hate. I'm

hopeful for a better life. Not a better life as it relates to money or

financial wealth, though I wouldn't push that aside. But a better life

234

as it relates to how we treat each other. I know my prayer may seem a little naive, but it's my prayer. Here's something and a question I have always been intrigued about. "Why does one race hate another race, when we're all supposed to be, in the eyes of God, made up from the same fabric?" Now I can talk about wars that have started over religion and ethnicity from many centuries past, because in some fashion, I believe these are some of the reasons behind hate. However, wars over ethnic cleansing and God's promise of who are the chosen are for another dream. I'm just asking a simple question. This question has haunted me in a country we revere as the country of the brave and the free. A country where the thought of exceptionalism seems to put her in a category all by itself. The biblical city upon the hill—AMERICA!

On its face, this country began on a lie: the White Anglo-Saxon ideology that suggests ALL men are equal and God is the one that will remove us from anything that is wrong, or bad. I don't want to get preachy, but someone please tell me why does one race hate another race? Is it because of the color of one's skin? Or is it because God suggests in the Bible, written by Anglo-Saxons, that the poor and slaves will always be among us, which gives the powerful Anglo-Saxon race the right to rule over and hate the least of these? The least of these includes everyone that is not of Anglo-Saxon descent.

It has just been within recent history, which suggest Jim Crow laws are supposed to be the thing of the past. However, we still have to deal with White cronyism and the good-old-boy system—a "New Order" so to speak. This system keeps us separated by race and economic status. We separate ourselves by political affiliation, money and anything that doesn't fit into the fabric of the Anglo way.

As an African-American male, I have to deal with the idea, not stated publicly any more, that I will never be as smart as my White counterpart. Is that true? Well, most of the White bosses I have ever had have had less education and creativity in the workforce than me. I listen to my spouse who is always fighting just to be recognized for her hard work. That's right, the hard work that comes from educating herself; because our society suggests education will merit you a special place in America. She has a master's degree from a great university and her boss has a high school diploma from a small

236

town in a southern state. She once told me he said just that, "Well, look at me…you have a masters and I have a high school diploma." Her interpretation of his suggestion was she needed to recognize his Whiteness or else.

Here's another question. Why, as African-Americans, are we now so upset with law enforcement? I have been affiliated in some form or fashion in the law enforcement arena my whole working career. Why do we think an institution like law enforcement will change how they do business of profiling when they have been doing business in a discriminatory fashion for the last 100 years? I'll just go back a few years, the Jim Crow era—you mean to tell me you don't remember seeing, or if you were too young to remember, reading in history books the high-pressure water hydrants, and dogs being released on African-Americans for doing something the Constitution gives ALL American the right to do—protest! I promise it's in the Constitution. Amendment I: "Congress shall make no law respecting an establishment of religion, or prohibiting the free exercise thereof; or abridging the freedom of **SPEECH,** or of the press, or the **RIGHT OF THE PEOPLE PEACEABLY TO**

237

ASSEMBLE, AND TO PETITION THE GOVERNMENT FOR A REDRESS OF GRIEVANCES." See, I told you it's written not by African-Americans, but by the framers of the constitution, who were ALL White men. So, does this amendment only apply to White America? This hatred of the African-American race has been around for a long time, it's a systemic culture, not some new phenomena. It bothers me when White people suggest because the election of the first African-American President, we should all hold hands and sing, "Kum-ba-yah My Lord." These same people who suggest this won't even acknowledge this brilliant Harvard graduate as president. They also won't acknowledge he is a true African-American—50 percent White and 50 percent Black. The funny thing is even Black people have bought into this ridiculous idea. Science will disprove this every time. The human DNA is made up of X and Y chromosomes—which mean we get half from our mother and the other half from our father.

Whether it is police brutality against people of color, or someone saying something stupid about Muslims (as if all Muslims are a part or have an affiliation with ISIS) and posting it on Facebook, or any

238

other social media site, technology has exposed hatred. The fact is if we are going to suggest ALL Muslims are affiliated with ISIS, then we must also suggest ALL Christians are affiliated with the KKK. Technology has now exposed incidents of Black youth being shot for just being black. Not that this hasn't been going on for a while, its just technology has provided another outlet for the many injustices to be seen. Did Trayvon Martin, Michael Brown, or many other Black youths have to die because of hate? No, I don't think so. As I jot down my limited viewpoint on why one race hates another race, I must realize that answering this question is hard and there is no straightforward answer. We live in a large and complex world, where race, money and influence are the true culprits.

My story is a fantasy story—a fiction. It's a story that reference true facts as they relate to race, but overall—this story came from a dream I had. A story of "What If?" Racism is deep rooted. I understand there will never be an eradication of racism, no more than the existence of Santa Clause, Easter Bunny or the Tooth Fairy. However, I am still hopeful we can get along and treat people according to how they deserve to be treated. I would be remiss if I didn't say a lot of the problems within the African-American community are promulgated by other African-Americans. In no way will I ever suggest blatant racism from our Caucasian brothers and sisters doesn't exist in our community. Job discrimination, profiling, and a host of other things that keep this racial train of injustice moving full speed ahead. I'm just noting, we as African-Americans can do a better job of policing ourselves. Also, we as African-Americans must acknowledge if it weren't for the strong white abolitionists and civil rights supporters like Mary Prince, Thomas Clarkson, James Stephen, James Ramsey and many more, who took up the fight against racial injustice and even died for the cause, we would not have come this far.

Willie Lynch was my friend, not because he mapped out a manifesto on how to keep the slave, or African-American in check even in the 21st century and beyond. Willie Lynch is my friend because it's the Willie Lynch's in the world that remind us we still have a long way to go to quall the many injustices within the African-American and Brown community.

THE END

www.ingramcontent.com/pod-product-compliance
Lightning Source LLC
Chambersburg PA
CBHW071149170626
46809CB00002B/834